MALONE DIES

SAMUEL BECKETT

MALONE DIES

a novel translated from the French
by the author

CALDER AND BOYARS
London

First published in Great Britain in 1958 by
John Calder (Publishers) Ltd.

Reprinted in 1968 by Calder & Boyars Ltd.,
18 Brewer Street, London, W.1

*Printed in Great Britain by
Taylor Garnett Evans & Co. Ltd.,
Watford*

MALONE DIES

I SHALL SOON BE QUITE DEAD AT LAST IN SPITE OF ALL. PERhaps next month. Then it will be the month of April or of May. For the year is still young, a thousand little signs tell me so. Perhaps I am wrong, perhaps I shall survive Saint John the Baptist's Day and even the Fourteenth of July, festival of freedom. Indeed I would not put it past me to pant on to the Transfiguration, not to speak of the Assumption. But I do not think so, I do not think I am wrong in saying that these rejoicings will take place in my absence, this year. I have that feeling, I have had it now for some days, and I credit it. But in what does it differ from those that have abused me ever since I was born? No, that is the kind of bait I do not rise to any more, my need for prettiness is gone. I could die to-day, if I wished, merely by making a little effort, if I could wish, if I could make an effort. But it is just as well to let myself die, quietly, without rushing things. Something must have changed. I will not weigh upon the balance any more, one way or the other. I shall be neutral and inert. No difficulty there. Throes are the only trouble, I must be on my guard against throes. But I am less given to them now, since coming here. Of course I still have my little fits of impatience, from time to time, I must be on my guard against them, for the next fortnight or three weeks. Without exaggeration to be sure, quietly crying and laughing, without working myself up into a state. Yes, I shall be natural at last, I shall suffer more, then less, without drawing any conclusions, I shall pay less heed to myself, I shall be neither hot nor cold any more, I shall be tepid, I shall die tepid, without enthusiasm. I shall not watch myself die, that would

1

spoil everything. Have I watched myself live? Have I ever complained? Then why rejoice now? I am content, necessarily, but not to the point of clapping my hands. I was always content, knowing I would be repaid. There he is now, my old debtor. Shall I then fall on his neck? I shall not answer any more questions. I shall even try not to ask myself any more. While waiting I shall tell myself stories, if I can. They will not be the same kind of stories as hitherto, that is all. They will be neither beautiful nor ugly, they will be calm, there will be no ugliness or beauty or fever in them any more, they will be almost lifeless, like the teller. What was that I said? It does not matter. I look forward to their giving me great satisfaction, some satisfaction. I am satisfied, there, I have enough, I am repaid, I need nothing more. Let me say before I go any further that I forgive nobody. I wish them all an atrocious life and then the fires and ice of hell and in the execrable generations to come an honoured name. Enough for this evening.

This time I know where I am going, it is no longer the ancient night, the recent night. Now it is a game, I am going to play. I never knew how to play, till now. I longed to, but I knew it was impossible. And yet I often tried. I turned on all the lights, I took a good look all round, I began to play with what I saw. People and things ask nothing better than to play, certain animals too. All went well at first, they all came to me, pleased that someone should want to play with them. If I said, Now I need a hunchback, immediately one came running, proud as punch of his fine hunch that was going to perform. It did not occur to him that I might have to ask him to undress. But it was not long before I found myself alone, in the dark. That is why I gave up trying to play and took to myself for ever shapelessness and speechlessness, incurious wondering, darkness, long stumbling with outstretched arms, hiding. Such is the earnestness from which, for nearly a century now, I have never been able to depart. From now on it will be different. I shall never do anything any more from now on but play. No, I must not begin with an exaggeration. But I shall play a great part of the time, from now on, the greater part, if I can. But perhaps I shall not succeed any better than hitherto. Perhaps as hitherto I shall find myself abandoned, in the dark, without anything to play with. Then I shall play with myself. To have been able to conceive such a plan is encouraging.

I must have thought about my time-table during the night. I think I shall be able to tell myself four stories, each one on a different theme. One about a man, another about a woman, a third about a thing and finally one about an animal, a bird probably. I think that is everything. Perhaps I shall put the man and the woman in the same story, there is so little difference between a man and a woman, between mine I mean. Perhaps I shall not have time to finish. On the other hand perhaps I shall finish too soon. There I am back at my old aporetics. Is that the word? I don't know. It does not matter if I do not finish. But if I finish too soon? That does not matter either. For then I shall speak of the things that remain in my possession, that is a thing I have always wanted to do. It will be a kind of inventory. In any case that is a thing I must leave to the very last moment, so as to be sure of not having made a mistake. In any case that is a thing I shall certainly do, no matter what happens. It will not take me more than a quarter of an hour at the most. That is to say it could take me longer, if I wished. But should I be short of time, at the last moment, then a brief quarter of an hour would be all I should need to draw up my inventory. My desire is henceforward to be clear, without being finical. I have always wanted that too. It is obvious I may suddenly expire, at any moment. Would it not then be better for me to speak of my possessions without further delay? Would not that be wiser? And then if necessary at the last moment correct any inaccuracies. That is what reason counsels. But reason has not much hold on me, just now. All things run together to encourage me. But can I really resign myself to the possibility of my dying without leaving an inventory behind?

There I am back at my old quibbles. Presumably I can, since I intend to take the risk. All my life long I have put off this reckoning, saying, Too soon, too soon. Well it is still too soon. All my life long I have dreamt of the moment when, edified at last, in so far as one can be before all is lost, I might draw the line and make the tot. This moment seems now at hand. I shall not lose my head on that account. So first of all my stories and then, last of all, if all goes well, my inventory. And I shall begin, that they may plague me no more, with the man and woman. That will be the first story, there is not matter there for two. There will therefore be only three stories after all, that one, then the one about the animal, then the one about the thing, a stone probably. That is all very clear. Then I shall deal with my possessions. If after all that I am still alive I shall take the necessary steps to ensure my not having made a mistake. So much for that. I used not to know where I was going, but I knew I would arrive, I knew there would be an end to the long blind road. What half-truths, my God. No matter. It is playtime now. I find it hard to get used to that idea. The old fog calls. Now the case is reversed, the way well charted and little hope of coming to its end. But I have high hopes. What am I doing now, I wonder, losing time or gaining it? I have also decided to remind myself briefly of my present state before embarking on my stories. I think this is a mistake. It is a weakness. But I shall indulge in it. I shall play with all the more ardour afterwards. And it will be a pendant to the inventory. Aesthetics are therefore on my side, at least a certain kind of aesthetics. For I shall have to become earnest again to be able to speak of my possessions. There it is then divided into five, the time that remains. Into five what? I don't know. Everything divides into itself, I suppose. If I start trying to think again I shall make a mess of my decease. I must say there is something very attractive about such a prospect. But I am on my guard. For the past few days I have been finding something attractive about everything. To return to the five. Present state, three stories, inventory, there. An occasional interlude is to be feared. A full programme. I shall not deviate from it any further than I must. So much for that. I feel I am making a great mistake. No matter.

Present state. This room seems to be mine. I can find no other explanation to my being left in it. All this time. Unless it be at the behest of one of the powers that be. That is hardly likely. Why should the powers have changed in their attitude towards me? It is better to adopt the simplest explanation, even if it is not simple, even if it does not explain very much. A bright light is not necessary, a taper is all one needs to live in strangeness, if it faithfully burns. Perhaps I came in for the room on the death of whoever was in it before me. I enquire no further in any case. It is not a room in a hospital, or in a madhouse, I can feel that. I have listened at different hours of the day and night and never heard anything suspicious or unusual, but always the peaceful sounds of men at large, getting up, lying down, preparing food, coming and going, weeping and laughing, or nothing at all, no sounds at all. And when I look out of the window it is clear to me, from certain signs, that I am not in a house of rest in any sense of the word. No, this is just a plain private room apparently, in what appears to be a plain ordinary house. I do not remember how I got here. In an ambulance perhaps, a vehicle of some kind certainly. One day I found myself here, in the bed. Having probably lost consciousness somewhere, I benefit by a hiatus in my recollections, not to be resumed until I recovered my senses, in this bed. As to the events that led up to my fainting and to which I can hardly have been oblivious, at the time, they have left no discernible trace, on my mind. But who has not experienced such lapses? They are common after drunkenness. I have often amused myself with trying to invent them, those same lost events. But without succeeding in amusing myself really. But what is the last thing I remember, I could start from there, before I came to my senses again here? That too is lost. I was walking certainly, all my life I have been walking, except the

5

first few months and since I have been here. But at the end of the day I did not know where I had been or what my thoughts had been. What then could I be expected to remember, and with what? I remember a mood. My young days were more varied, such as they come back to me, in fits and starts. I did not know my way about so well then. I have lived in a kind of coma. The loss of consciousness for me was never any great loss. But perhaps I was stunned with a blow, on the head, in a forest perhaps, yes, now that I speak of a forest I vaguely remember a forest. All that belongs to the past. Now it is the present I must establish, before I am avenged. It is an ordinary room. I have little experience of rooms, but this one seems quite ordinary to me. The truth is, if I did not feel myself dying, I could well believe myself dead, expiating my sins, or in one of heaven's mansions. But I feel at last that the sands are running out, which would not be the case if I were in heaven, or in hell. Beyond the grave, the sensation of being beyond the grave was stronger with me six months ago. Had it been foretold to me that one day I should feel myself living as I do to-day, I should have smiled. It would not have been noticed, but I would have known I was smiling. I remember them well, these last few days, they have left me more memories than the thirty thousand odd that went before. The reverse would have been less surprising. When I have completed my inventory, if my death is not ready for me then, I shall write my memoirs. That's funny, I have made a joke. No matter. There is a cupboard I have never looked into. My possessions are in a corner, in a little heap. With my long stick I can rummage in them, draw them to me, send them back. My bed is by the window. I lie turned towards it most of the time. I see roofs and sky, a glimpse of street too, if I crane. I do not see any fields or hills. And yet they are near. But are they near? I don't know. I do not see the sea either, but I hear it when it is high. I can see into a room of the house across the way. Queer things go on there sometimes, people are queer. Perhaps these are abnormal. They must see me too, my big shaggy head up against the window-pane. I never had so much hair as now, nor so long, I say it without fear of contradiction. But at night they do not see me, for I never have a light. I have studied the stars a little here. But I cannot find my way about among them. Gazing at them one night I suddenly saw myself in London. Is it possible I got as far as London? And what have stars to do with that city? The moon on the other hand has grown familiar, I am well familiar now with her changes of aspect and orbit, I know more or less the hours of the night when I may look for her in the sky and the nights when she will not come. What else? The clouds. They are varied, very varied. And all sorts of birds. They come and perch on the window-sill, asking for food! It is touching. They rap on the window-pane, with their beaks. I never give them anything. But they still come. What are they waiting for? They are not vultures. Not only am I left here, but I am looked after! This is how it is done now. The door half opens, a hand puts a dish on the little table left there for that purpose, takes away the dish of the previous day, and the door closes again. This is done for me every day, at the same time probably. When I want to eat I hook the table with my stick and draw it to me. It is on castors, it comes squeaking and lurching towards me. When I need it no longer I send it back to its place by the door. It is soup. They must know I am toothless. I eat it one time out of two, out of three, on an average. When my chamber-pot is full I put it on the table, beside the dish. Then I go twenty-four hours without a pot. No, I have two pots. They have thought of everything. I am naked in the bed, in the blankets, whose number I increase and diminish as the seasons come and go. I am never hot, never cold. I don't wash, but I don't get dirty. If I get dirty somewhere I rub the part with my finger wet with spittle. What matters is to eat and excrete. Dish and pot, dish and pot, these are the poles. In the beginning it was different. The woman came right into the room, bustled about, enquired about my needs, my wants. I succeeded in the end in getting them into her head, my needs and my wants. It was not easy. She did not understand. Until the day I found the terms, the accents, that fitted her. All that must be half imagination. It was she who got me this long stick. It has a hook at one end. Thanks to it I can control the furthest recesses of my abode. How great is my debt to sticks! So great that I almost forget the blows they have transferred to me. She is an old woman. I don't know why she is good to me. Yes, let us call it goodness, without quibbling. For her it is certainly goodness. I believe her to be even older than I. But rather less well preserved, in spite of her mobility. Perhaps she goes with the room, in a manner of speaking. In that case she does not call for separate study. But it is conceivable that she does what she does out of sheer charity, or moved with regard to me by a less general feeling of compassion or affection. Nothing is impossible, I cannot keep on denying it much longer. But it is more convenient to suppose that when I came in for the room I came in for her too. All I see of her now is the gaunt hand and part of the sleeve. Not even that, not even that. Perhaps she is dead, having predeceased me, perhaps now it is another's hand that lays and clears my little table. I don't know how long I have been here, I must have said so. All I know is that I was very old already before I found myself here. I call myself an octogenarian, but I cannot prove it. Perhaps I am only a quinquagenarian, or a quadragenarian. It is ages since I counted them, my years I mean. I know the year of my birth, I have not forgotten that, but I do not know what year I have got to now. But I think I have been here for some very considerable time. For there is nothing the various seasons can do to me, within the shelter of these walls, that I do not know. That is not to be learnt in one year or two. In a flicker of my lids whole days have flown. Does anything remain to be said? A few words about myself perhaps. My body is what is called, unadvisedly perhaps, impotent. There is virtually nothing it can do. Sometimes I miss not being able to crawl around any more. But I am not much given to nostalgia. My arms, once they are in position, can exert a certain force. But I find it hard to guide them. Perhaps the red nucleus has faded. I tremble a little, but only a little. The groaning of the bedstead is part of my life, I would not like it to cease, I mean I would not like it to decrease. It is on my back, that is to say prostrate, no, supine, that I feel best, least bony. I lie on my back, but my cheek is on the pillow. I have only to open my eyes to have them begin again, the sky and smoke of mankind. My sight and hearing are very bad, on the vast main no light but reflected gleams. All my senses are trained full on me, me. Dark and silent and stale, I am no prey for them. I am far from the sounds of blood and breath, immured. I shall not speak of my sufferings. Cowering deep down among them I feel nothing. It is there I die, unbeknown to my stupid flesh. That which is seen, that which cries and writhes, my witless remains. Somewhere in this turmoil thought struggles on, it too wide of the mark. It too seeks me, as it always has, where I am not to be found. It too cannot be quiet. On others let it wreak its dying rage, and leave me in peace. Such would seem to be my present state.

The man's name is Saposcat. Like his father's. Christian name? I don't know. He will not need one. His friends call him Sapo. What friends? I don't know. A few words about the boy. This cannot be avoided.

He was a precocious boy. He was not good at his lessons, neither could he see the use of them. He attended his classes with his mind elsewhere, or blank.

He attended his classes with his mind elsewhere. He liked sums, but not the way they were taught. What he liked was the manipulation of concrete numbers. All calculation seemed to him idle in which the nature of the unit was not specified. He made a practice, alone and in company, of mental arithmetic. And the figures then marshalling in his mind thronged it with colours and with forms.

What tedium.

He was the eldest child of poor and sickly parents. He often heard them talk of what they ought to do in order to have better health and more money. He was struck each time by the vagueness of these palavers and not surprised that they never led to anything. His father was a salesman, in a shop. He used to say to his wife, I really must find work for the evenings and the Saturday afternoon. He added, faintly, And the Sunday. His wife would answer, But if you do any more work you'll fall ill. And Mr. Saposcat had to allow that he would indeed be ill-advised to forego his Sunday rest. These people at least are grown up. But his health was not so poor that he could not work in the evenings of the week and on the Saturday afternoon. At what, said his wife, work at what? Perhaps secretarial work of some kind, he said. And who will look after the garden? said his wife. The life of the Saposcats was full of axioms, of which one at least established the criminal absurdity of a garden without roses and with its paths and lawns uncared for. I might perhaps grow vegetables, he said. They cost less to buy, said his wife. Sapo marvelled at these conversations. Think of the price of manure, said his mother. And in the silence which followed Mr. Saposcat applied his mind, with the earnestness he brought to everything he did, to the high price of manure which prevented him from supporting his family in greater comfort, while his wife made ready to accuse herself, in her turn, of not doing all she might. But she was easily persuaded that she could not do more without exposing herself to the risk of dying before her time. Think of the doctor's fees we save, said Mr. Saposcat. And the chemist's bills, said his wife. Nothing remained but to envisage a smaller house. But we are cramped as it is, said Mrs. Saposcat. And it was an understood thing that they would be more and more so with every passing year until the day came when, the departure of the first-born compensating the arrival of the new-born, a kind of equilibrium would be attained. Then little by little the house would empty. And at last they would be all alone, with their memories. It would be

10

time enough then to move. He would be pensioned off, she at her last gasp. They would take a cottage in the country where, having no further need of manure, they could afford to buy it in cartloads. And their children, grateful for the sacrifices made on their behalf, would come to their assistance. It was in this atmosphere of unbridled dream that these conferences usually ended. It was as though the Saposcats drew the strength to live from the prospect of their impotence. But sometimes, before reaching that stage, they paused to consider the case of their first-born. What age is he now? asked Mr. Saposcat. His wife provided the information, it being understood that this was of her province. She was always wrong. Mr. Saposcat took over the erroneous figure, murmuring it over and over to himself as though it were a question of the rise in price of some indispensable commodity, such as butcher's meat. And at the same time he sought in the appearance of his son some alleviation of what he had just heard. Was it at least a nice sirloin? Sapo looked at his father's face, sad, astonished, loving, disappointed, confident in spite of all. Was it on the cruel flight of the years he brooded, or on the time it was taking his son to command a salary? Sometimes he stated wearily his regret that his son should not be more eager to make himself useful about the place. It is better for him to prepare his examinations, said his wife. Starting from a given theme their minds laboured in unison. They had no conversation properly speaking. They made use of the spoken word in much the same way as the guard of a train makes use of his flags, or of his lantern. Or else they said, This is where we get down. And their son once signalled, they wondered sadly if it was not the mark of superior minds to fail miserably at the written paper and cover themselves with ridicule at the viva voce. They were not always content to gape in silence at the same landcape. At least his health is good, said Mr. Saposcat. Not all that, said his wife. But no definite disease, said Mr. Saposcat. A nice thing that would be, at his age, said his wife. They did not know why he was committed to a liberal profession. That was yet another thing that went without saying. It was therefore impossible he should be unfitted for it. They thought of him as a doctor for preference. He will look after us when we are old, said Mrs. Saposcat. And her husband replied, I see him rather as a surgeon, as though after a certain age people were inoperable.

What tedium. And I call that playing. I wonder if I am not talking yet again about myself. Shall I be incapable, to the end, of lying on any other subject? I feel the old dark gathering, the solitude preparing, by which I know myself, and the call of that ignorance which might be noble and is mere poltroonery. Already I forget what I have said. That is not how to play. Soon I shall not know where Sapo comes from, nor what he hopes. Perhaps I had better abandon this story and go on to the second, or even the third, the one about the stone. No, it would be the same thing. I must simply be on my guard, reflecting on what I have said before I go on and stopping, each time disaster threatens, to look at myself as I am. That is just what I wanted to avoid. But there seems to be no other solution. After that mud-bath I shall be better able to endure a world unsullied by my presence. What a way to reason. My eyes, I shall open my eyes, look at the little heap of my possessions, give my body the old orders I know it cannot obey, turn to my spirit gone to rack and ruin, spoil my agony the better to live it out, far already from the world that parts at last its labia and lets me go.

I have tried to reflect on the beginning of my story. There are things I do not understand. But nothing to signify. I can go on.

Sapo had no friends—no, that won't do.

Sapo was on good terms with his little friends, though they did not exactly love him. The dolt is seldom solitary. He boxed and wrestled well, was fleet of foot, sneered at his teachers and sometimes even gave them impertinent answers. Fleet of foot? Well well. Pestered with questions one day he cried, Haven't I told you I don't know! Much of his free time he spent confined in school doing impositions and often he did not get home before eight o'clock at night. He submitted with philosophy to these vexations. But he would not let himself be struck. The first time an exasperated master threatened him with a cane, Sapo snatched it from his hand and threw it out of the window, which was closed, for it was winter. This was enough to justify his expulsion. But Sapo was not expelled, either then or later. I must try and discover, when I have time to think about it quietly, why Sapo was not expelled when he so richly deserved to be. For I want as little as possible of darkness in his story. A little darkness, in itself, at the time, is nothing. You think no more about it and you go on. But I know what darkness is, it accumulates, thickens, then suddenly bursts and drowns everything.

I have not been able to find out why Sapo was not expelled. I shall have to leave this question open. I try not to be glad. I shall make haste to put a safe remove between him and this incomprehensible indulgence, I shall make him live as though he had been punished according to his deserts. We shall turn our backs on this little cloud, but we shall not let it out of our sight. It will not cover the sky without our knowing, we shall not suddenly raise our eyes, far from help, far from shelter, to a sky as black as ink. That is what I have decided. I see no other solution. It is the best I can do.

At the age of fourteen he was a plump rosy boy. His wrists and ankles were thick, which made his mother say that one day he would be even bigger than his father. Curious deduction. But the most striking thing about him was his big round head horrid with flaxen hair as stiff and straight as the bristles of a brush. Even his teachers could not help thinking he had a remarkable head and they were all the more irked by their failure to get anything into it. His father would say, when in good humour, One of these days he will astonish us all. It was thanks to Sapo's skull that he was enabled to hazard this opinion and, in defiance of the facts and against his better judgment, to revert to it from time to time. But he could not endure the look in Sapo's eyes and went out of his way not to meet it. He has your eyes, his wife would say. Then Mr. Saposcat chafed to be alone, in order to inspect his eyes in the mirror. They were palest blue. Just a shade lighter, said Mrs. Saposcat.

Sapo loved nature, took an interest

This is awful.

Sapo loved nature, took an interest in animals and plants and willingly raised his eyes to the sky, day and night. But he did not know how to look at all these things, the looks he rained upon them taught him nothing about them. He confused the birds with one another, and the trees, and could not tell one crop from another crop. He did not associate the crocus with the spring nor the chrysanthemum with Michaelmas. The sun, the moon, the planets and the stars did not fill him with wonder. He was sometimes tempted by the knowledge of these strange things, sometimes beautiful, that he would have about him all his life. But from his ignorance of them he drew a kind of joy, as from all that went to swell the murmur, You are a simpleton. But he loved the flight of the hawk and could distinguish it from all others. He would stand rapt, gazing at the long pernings, the quivering poise, the wings lifted for the plummet drop, the wild reascent, fascinated by such extremes of need, of pride, of patience and solitude.

I shall not give up yet. I have finished my soup and sent back the little table to its place by the door. A light has just gone on in one of the two windows of the house across the way. By the two windows I mean those I can see always, without raising my head from the pillow. By this I do not mean the two windows in their entirety, but one in its entirety and part of the other. It is in this latter that the light has just gone on. For an instant I could see the woman coming and going. Then she drew the curtain. Until to-morrow I shall not see her again, her shadow perhaps from time to time. She does not always draw the curtain. The man has not yet come home. Home. I have demanded certain movements of my legs and even feet. I know them well and could feel the effort they made to obey. I have lived with them that little space of time, filled with drama, between the message received and the piteous response. To old dogs the hour comes when, whistled by their master setting forth with his stick at dawn, they cannot spring after him. Then they stay in their kennel, or in their basket, though they are not chained, and listen to the steps dying away. The man too is sad. But soon the pure air and the sun console him, he thinks no more about his old companion, until evening. The lights in his house bid him welcome home and a feeble barking makes him say, It is time I had him destroyed. There's a nice passage. Soon it will be even better, soon things will be better. I am going to rummage a little in my possessions. Then I shall put my head under the blankets. Then things will be better, for Sapo and for him who follows him, who asks nothing but to follow in his footsteps, by clear and endurable ways.

Sapo's phlegm, his silent ways, were not of a nature to please. In the midst of tumult, at school and at home, he remained motionless in his place, often standing, and gazed straight before him with eyes as pale and unwavering as a gull's. People wondered what he could brood on thus, hour after hour. His father supposed him a prey to the first flutterings of sex. At sixteen I was the same, he would say. At sixteen you were earning your living, said his wife. So I was, said Mr. Saposcat. But in the view of his teachers the signs were rather those of besottedness pure and simple. Sapo dropped his jaw and breathed through his mouth. It is not easy to see in virtue of what this expression is incompatible with erotic thoughts. But indeed his dream was less of girls than of himself, his own life, his life to be. That is more than enough to stop up the nose of a lucid and sensitive boy, and cause his jaw temporarily to sag. But it is time I took a little rest, for safety's sake.

I don't like those gull's eyes. They remind me of an old ship-wreck, I forget which. I know it is a small thing. But I am easily frightened now. I know those little phrases that seem so innocuous and, once you let them in, pollute the whole of speech. *Nothing is more real than nothing.* They rise up out of the pit and know no rest until they drag you down into its dark. But I am on my guard now.

Then he was sorry he had not learnt the art of thinking, beginning by folding back the second and third fingers the better to put the index on the subject and the little finger on the verb, in the way his teacher had shown him, and sorry he could make no meaning of the babel raging in his head, the doubts, desires, imaginings and dreads. And a little less well endowed with strength and courage he too would have abandoned and despaired of ever knowing what manner of being he was, and how he was going to live, and lived vanquished, blindly, in a mad world, in the midst of strangers.

From these reveries he emerged tired and pale, which confirmed his father's impression that he was the victim of lascivious speculations. He ought to play more games, he would say. We are getting on, getting on. They told me he would be a good athlete, said Mr. Saposcat, and now he is not on any team. His studies take up all his time, said Mrs. Saposcat. And he is always last, said Mr. Saposcat. He is fond of walking, said Mrs. Saposcat, the long walks in the country do him good. Then Mr. Saposcat wried his face, at the thought of his son's long solitary walks and the good they did him. And sometimes he was carried away to the point of saying, It might have been better to have put him to a trade. Whereupon it was usual, though not compulsory, for Sapo to go away, while his mother exclaimed, Oh Adrian, you have hurt his feelings!

We are getting on. Nothing is less like me than this patient, reasonable child, struggling all alone for years to shed a little light upon himself, avid of the least gleam, a stranger to the joys of darkness. Here truly is the air I needed, a lively tenuous air, far from the nourishing murk that is killing me. I shall never go back into this carcass except to find out its time. I want to be there a little before the plunge, close for the last time the old hatch on top of me, say goodbye to the holds where I have lived, go down with my refuge. I was always sentimental. But between now and then I have time to frolic, ashore, in the brave company I have always longed for, always searched for, and which would never have me. Yes, now my mind is easy, I know the game is won, I lost them all till now, but it's the last that counts. A very fine achievement I must say, or rather would, if I did not fear to contradict myself. Fear to contradict myself! If this continues it is myself I shall lose and the thousand ways that lead there. And I shall resemble the wretches famed in fable, crushed beneath the weight of their wish come true. And I even feel a strange desire come over me, the desire to know what I am doing, and why. So I near the goal I set myself in my young days and which prevented me from living. And on the threshold of being no more I succeed in being another. Very pretty.

The summer holidays. In the morning he took private lessons. You'll have us in the poorhouse, said Mrs. Saposcat. It's a good investment, said Mr. Saposcat. In the afternoon he left the house, with his books under his arm, on the pretext that he worked better in the open air, no, without a word. Once clear of the town he hid his books under a stone and ranged the countryside. It was the season when the labours of the peasants reach their paroxysm and the long bright days are too short for all there is to do. And often they took advantage

17

of the moon to make a last journey between the fields, perhaps far away, and the barn or threshing floor, or to overhaul the machines and get them ready for the impending dawn. The impending dawn.

I fell asleep. But I do not want to sleep. There is no time for sleep in my time-table. I do not want—no, I have no explanations to give. Coma is for the living. The living. They were always more than I could bear, all, no, I don't mean that, but groaning with tedium I watched them come and go, then I killed them, or took their place, or fled. I feel within me the glow of that old frenzy, but I know it will set me on fire no more. I stop everything and wait. Sapo stands on one leg, motionless, his strange eyes closed. The turmoil of the day freezes in a thousand absurd postures. The little cloud drifting before their glorious sun will darken the earth as long as I please.

Live and invent. I have tried. I must have tried. Invent. It is not the word. Neither is live. No matter. I have tried. While within me the wild beast of earnestness padded up and down, roaring, ravening, rending. I have done that. And all alone, well hidden, played the clown, all alone, hour after hour, motionless, often standing, spellbound, groaning. That's right, groan. I couldn't play. I turned till I was dizzy, clapped my hands, ran, shouted, saw myself winning, saw myself losing, rejoicing, lamenting. Then suddenly I threw myself on the playthings, if there were any, or on a child, to change his joy to howling, or I fled, to hiding. The grown-ups pursued me, the just, caught me, beat me, hounded me back into the round, the game, the jollity. For I was already in the toils of earnestness. That has been my disease. I was born grave as others syphilitic. And gravely I struggled to be grave no more, to live, to invent, I know what I mean. But at each fresh attempt I lost my head, fled to my shadows as to sanctuary, to his lap who can neither live nor suffer the sight of others living. I say living without knowing what it is. I tried to live without knowing what I was trying. Perhaps I have lived after all, without knowing. I wonder why I speak of all this. Ah yes, to relieve the tedium. Live and cause to live. There is no use indicting words, they are no shoddier than what they peddle. After the fiasco, the solace, the repose, I began again, to try and live, cause to live, be another, in myself, in another. How false all this is. No time now to explain. I began again. But little by little with a different aim, no longer in order to succeed, but in order to fail. Nuance. What I sought, when I struggled out of my hole, then aloft through the stinging air towards an inaccessible boon, was the rapture of vertigo, the letting go, the fall, the gulf, the relapse to darkness, to nothingness, to earnestness, to home, to him waiting for me always, who needed me and whom I needed, who took me in his arms and told me to stay with him always, who gave me·his place and watched over me, who suffered every time I left him, whom I have often made suffer and seldom contented, whom I have never seen. There I am forgetting myself again. My concern is not with me, but with another, far beneath me and whom I try to envy, of whose crass adventures I can now tell at last, I don't know how. Of myself I could never tell, any more than live or tell of others. How could I have, who never tried? To show myself now, on the point of vanishing, at the same time as the stranger, and by the same grace, that would be no ordinary last straw. Then live, long enough to feel, behind my closed eyes, other eyes close. What an end.

The market. The inadequacy of the exchanges between rural and urban areas had not escaped the excellent youth. He had mustered, on this subject, the following considerations, some perhaps close to, others no doubt far from, the truth.

In his country the problem—no, I can't do it.

The peasants. His visits to. I can't. Assembled in the farm-yard they watched him depart, on stumbling, wavering feet, as though they scarcely felt the ground. Often he stopped, stood tottering a moment, then suddenly was off again, in a new direction. So he went, limp, drifting, as though tossed by the earth. And when, after a halt, he started off again, it was like a big thistledown plucked by the wind from the place where it had settled. There is a choice of images.

I have rummaged a little in my things, sorting them out and drawing them over to me, to look at them. I was not far wrong in thinking that I knew them off, by heart, and could speak of them at any moment, without looking at them. But I wanted to make sure. It was well I did. For now I know that the image of these objects, with which I have lulled myself till now, though accurate in the main, was not completely so. And I should be sorry to let slip this unique occasion which seems to offer me the possibility of something suspiciously like a true statement at last. I might feel I had failed in my duty! I want this matter to be free from all trace of approximativeness. I want, when the great day comes, to be in a position to enounce clearly, without addition or omission, all that its interminable prelude had brought me and left me in the way of chattels personal. I presume it is an obsession.

I see then I had attributed to myself certain objects no longer in my possession, as far as I can see. But might they not have rolled behind a piece of furniture? That would surprise me. A boot, for example, can a boot roll behind a piece of furniture? And yet I see only one boot. And behind what piece of furniture? In this room, to the best of my knowledge, there is only one piece of furniture capable of intervening between me and my possessions, I refer to the cupboard. But it so cleaves to the wall, to the two walls, for it stands in the corner, that it seems part of them. It may be objected that my button-boot, for it was a kind of button-boot, is in the cupboard. I thought of that. But I have gone through it, my stick has gone through the cupboard, opening the doors, the drawers, for the first time perhaps, and rooting everywhere. And the cupboard, far from containing my boot, is empty. No, I am now without this boot, just as I am now without certain other objects of less value, which I thought I had preserved, among them a zinc ring that shone like silver. I note on the other hand, in the heap, the presence of two or three objects I had quite forgotten and one of which at least, the bowl of a pipe, strikes no chord in my memory. I do not remember ever having smoked a tobacco-pipe. I remember the soap-pipe with which, as a child, I used to blow bubbles, an odd bubble. Never mind, this bowl is now mine, wherever it comes from. A number of my treasures are derived from the same source. I also discovered a little packet tied up in age-yellowed newspaper. It reminds me of something, but of what? I drew it over beside the bed and felt it with the knob of my stick. And my hand understood, it understood softness and lightness, better I think than if it had touched the thing directly, fingering it and weighing it in its palm. I resolved, I don't know why, not to undo it. I sent it back into the corner, with the rest. I shall speak of it again perhaps, when the time comes. I shall say, I can hear myself already, Item, a little packet, soft, and light as a feather, tied up in newspaper. It will be my little mystery, all my own. Perhaps it is a lack of rupees. Or a lock of hair.

I told myself too that I must make better speed. True lives do not tolerate this excess of circumstance. It is there the demon lurks, like the gonococcus in the folds of the prostate. My time is limited. It is thence that one fine day, when all nature smiles and shines, the rack lets loose its black unforgettable cohorts and sweeps away the blue for ever. My situation is truly delicate. What fine things, what momentous things, I am going to miss through fear, fear of falling back into the old error, fear of not finishing in time, fear of revelling, for the last time, in a last outpouring of misery, impotence and hate. The forms are many in which the unchanging seeks relief from its formlessness. Ah yes, I was always subject to the deep thought, especially in the spring of the year. That one had been nagging at me for the past five minutes. I venture to hope there will be no more, of that depth. After all it is not important not to finish, there are worse things than velleities. But is that the point? Quite likely. All I ask is that the last of mine, as long as it lasts, should have living for its theme, that is all, I know what I mean. If it begins to run short of life I shall feel it. All I ask is to know, before I abandon him whose life has so well begun, that my death and mine alone prevents him from living on, from winning, losing, joying, suffering, rotting and dying, and that even had I lived he would have waited, before he died, for his body to be dead. That is what you might call taking a reef in your sails.

My body does not yet make up its mind. But I fancy it weighs heavier on the bed, flattens and spreads. My breath, when it comes back, fills the room with its din, though my chest moves no more than a sleeping child's. I open my eyes and gaze unblinkingly and long at the night sky. So a tiny tot I gaped, first at the novelties, then at the antiquities. Between it and me the pane, misted and smeared with the filth of years. I should like to breathe on it, but it is too far away. It is such a night as Kaspar David Friedrich loved, tempestuous and bright. That name that comes back to me, those names. The clouds scud, tattered by the wind, across a limpid ground. If I had the patience to wait I would see the moon. But I have not. Now that I have looked I hear the wind. I close my eyes and it mingles with my breath. Words and images run riot in my head, pursuing, flying, clashing, merging, endlessly. But beyond this tumult there is a great calm, and a great indifference, never really to be troubled by anything again. I turn a little on my side, press my mouth against the pillow, and my nose, crush against the pillow my old hairs now no doubt as white as snow, pull the blanket over my head. I feel, deep down in my trunk, I cannot be more explicit, pains that seem new to me. I think they are chiefly in my back. They have a kind of rhythm, they even have a kind of little tune. They are bluish. How bearable all that is, my God. My head is almost facing the wrong way,

22

like a bird's. I part my lips, now I have the pillow in my mouth. I have, I have. I suck. The search for myself is ended. I am buried in the world, I knew I would find my place there one day, the old world cloisters me, victorious. I am happy, I knew I would be happy one day. But I am not wise. For the wise thing now would be to let go, at this instant of happiness. And what do I do? I go back again to the light, to the fields I so longed to love, to the sky all astir with little white clouds as white and light as snowflakes, to the life I could never manage, through my own fault perhaps, through pride, or pettiness, but I don't think so. The beasts are at pasture, the sun warms the rocks and makes them glitter. Yes, I leave my happiness and go back to the race of men too, they come and go, often with burdens. Perhaps I have judged them ill, but I don't think so, I have not judged them at all. All I want now is to make a last effort to understand, to begin to understand, how such creatures are possible. No, it is not a question of understanding. Of what then? I don't know. Here I go none the less, mistakenly. Night, storm and sorrow, and the catalepsies of the soul, this time I shall see that they are good. The last word is not yet said between me and—yes, the last word is said. Perhaps I simply want to hear it said again. Just once again. No, I want nothing.

The Lamberts. The Lamberts found it difficult to live, I mean to make ends meet. There was the man, the woman and two children, a boy and a girl. There at least is something that admits of no controversy. The father was known as Big Lambert, and big he was indeed. He had married his young cousin and was still with her. This was his third or fourth marriage. He had other children here and there, grown men and women imbedded deep in life, hoping for nothing more, from themselves or from others. They helped him, each one according to his means, or the humour of the moment, out of gratitude towards him but for whom they had never seen the light of day, or saying, with indulgence, If it had not been he it would have been someone else. Big Lambert had not a tooth in his head and smoked his cigarettes in a cigarette-holder, while regretting his pipe. He was highly thought of as a bleeder and disjointer of pigs and greatly sought after, I exaggerate, in that capacity. For his fee was lower than the butcher's, and he had even been known to demand no more, in return for his services, than a lump of gammon or a pig's cheek. How plausible all that is. He often spoke of his father with respect and tenderness. His like will not be seen again, he used to say, once I am gone. He must have said this in other words. His great days then fell in December and January, and from February onwards he waited impatiently for the return of that season, the principal event of which is unquestionably the Saviour's birth, in a stable, while wondering if he would be spared till then. Then he would set forth, hugging under his arm, in their case, the great knives so lovingly whetted before the fire the night before, and in his pocket, wrapped in paper, the apron destined to protect his Sunday suit while he worked. And at the thought that he, Big Lambert, was on his way towards that distant homestead where all was in readiness for his coming, and that in spite of his great age he was still needed, and his methods preferred to those of younger men, then his old heart exulted. From these expeditions he reached home late in the night, drunk and exhausted by the long road and the emotions of the day. And for days afterwards he could speak of nothing but the pig he had just dispatched, I would say into the other world if I was not aware that pigs have none but this, to the great affliction of his family. But they did not dare protest, for they feared him. Yes, at an age when most people cringe and cower, as if to apologize for still being present, Lambert was feared and in a position to do as he pleased. And even his young wife had abandoned all hope of bringing him to heel, by means of her cunt, that trump card of young wives. For she knew what he would do to her if she did not open it to him. And he even insisted on her making things easy for him, in ways that often appeared to her exorbitant. And at the least show of rebellion on her part he would run to the wash-house and come back with the battle and beat her until she came round to a better way of thinking. All this by the way. And to return to our pigs, Lambert continued to expatiate, to his near and dear ones, of an evening, while the lamp burned low, on the specimen he had just slaughtered, until the day he was summoned to slaughter another. Then all his conversation was of this new pig, so unlike the other in every respect, so quite unlike, and yet at bottom the same. For all pigs are alike, when you get to know their little ways, struggle, squeal, bleed, squeal, struggle, bleed, squeal and faint away, in more or less the same way exactly, a way that is all their own and could never be imitated by a lamb, for example, or a kid. But once March was out Big Lambert recovered his calm and became his silent self again.

The son, or heir, was a great strapping lad with terrible teeth.

The farm. The farm was in a hollow, flooded in winter and in summer burnt to a cinder. The way to it lay through a fine meadow. But this fine meadow did not belong to the Lamberts, but to other peasants living at a distance. There jonquils and narcissi bloomed in extraordinary profusion, at the appropriate season. And there at nightfall, stealthily, Big Lambert turned loose his goats.

Strange to say this gift that Lambert possessed when it came to sticking pigs seemed of no help to him when it came to rearing them, and it was seldom his own exceeded nine stone. Clapped into a tiny sty on the day of its arrival, in the month of April, it remained there until the day of its death, on Christmas Eve. For Lambert persisted in dreading for his pigs, though every passing year proved him wrong, the thinning effects of exercise. Daylight and fresh air he dreaded for them too. And it was finally a weak pig, blind and lean, that he lay on its back in the box, having tied its legs, and killed, indignantly but without haste, upraiding it the while for its ingratitude, at the top of his voice. For he could not or would not understand that the pig was not to blame, but he himself, who had coddled it unduly. And he persisted in his error.

Dead world, airless, waterless. That's it, reminisce. Here and there, in the bed of a crater, the shadow of a withered lichen. And nights of three hundred hours. Dearest of lights, wan, pitted, least fatuous of lights. That's it, babble. How long can it have lasted? Five minutes? Ten minutes? Yes, no more, not much more. But my sliver of sky is silvery with it yet. In the old days I used to count, up to three hundred, four hundred, and with other things too, the showers, the bells, the chatter of the sparrows at dawn, or with nothing, for no reason, for the sake of counting, and then I divided, by sixty. That passed the time, I was time, I devoured the world. Not now, any more. A man changes. As he gets on.

In the filthy kitchen, with its earth floor, Sapo had his place, by the window. Big Lambert and his son left their work, came and shook his hand, then went away, leaving him with the mother and the daughter. But they too had their work, they too went away and left him, alone. There was so much work, so little time, so few hands. The woman, pausing an instant between two tasks, or in the midst of one, flung up her arms and, in the same breath, unable to sustain their great weight, let them fall again. Then she began to toss them about in a way difficult to describe, and not easy to understand. The movements resembled those, at once frantic and slack, of an arm shaking a duster, or a rag, to rid it of its dust. And so rapid was the trepidation of the limp, empty hands that there seemed to be four or five at the end of each arm, instead of the usual one. At the same time angry unanswerable questions, such as, What's the use? fell from her lips. Her hair came loose and fell about her face. It was thick, grey and dirty, for she had no time to tend it, and her face was pale and thin and as though gouged with worry and its attendant rancours. The bosom—no, what matters is the head and then the hands it calls to its help before all else, that clasp, wring, then sadly resume their labour, lifting the old inert objects and changing their position, bringing them closer together and moving them further apart. But this pantomime and these ejaculations were not intended for any living person. For every day and several times a day she gave way to them, within doors and without. Then she little cared whether she was observed or not, whether what she was doing was urgent or could wait, no, but she dropped everything and began to cry out and gesticulate, the last of all the living as likely as not and dead to what was going on about her. Then she fell silent and stood stockstill a moment, before resuming whatever it was she had abandoned or setting about some new task. Sapo remained alone, by the window, the bowl of goat's milk on the table before him, forgotten. It was summer. The room was dark in spite of the door and window open on the great outer light. Through these narrow openings, far apart, the light poured, lit up a little space, then died, undiffused. It had no steadfastness, no assurance of lasting as long as day lasted. But it entered at every moment, renewed from without, entered and died at every moment, devoured by the dark. And at the least abatement of the inflow the room grew darker and darker until nothing in it was visible any more. For the dark had triumphed. And Sapo, his face turned towards an earth so resplendent that it hurt his eyes, felt at his back and all about him the unconquerable dark, and it licked the light on his face. Sometimes abruptly he turned to face it, letting it envelop and pervade him, with a kind of relief. Then he heard more clearly the sounds of those at work, the daughter calling to her goats, the father cursing his mule. But silence was in the heart of the dark, the silence of dust and the things that would never stir, if left alone. And the ticking of the invisible alarm-clock was as the voice of that silence which, like the dark, would one day triumph too. And then all would be still and dark and all things at rest for ever at last. Finally he took from his pocket the few poor gifts he had brought, laid them on the table and went. But it sometimes happened, before he decided to go, before he went rather, for there was no decision, that a hen, taking advantage of the open door, would venture into the room. No sooner had she crossed the threshold than she paused, one leg hooked up under her breech, her head on one side, blinking, anxious. Then, reassured, she advanced a little further, jerkily, with concertina neck. It was a grey hen, perhaps the grey hen. Sapo got to know her well and, it seemed to him, to be well known by her. If he rose to go she did not fly into a flutter. But perhaps there were several hens, all grey and so alike in other respects that Sapo's eye, avid of resemblances, could not tell between them. Sometimes she was followed by a second, a third and even a fourth, bearing no likeness to her, and but little to one another, in the matter of plumage and entasis. These showed more confidence than the grey, who had led the way and come to no harm. They shone an instant in the light, grew dimmer and dimmer as they advanced, and finally vanished. Silent at first, fearing to betray their presence, they began gradually to scratch and cluck, for contentment, and to relax their soughing feathers. But often the grey hen came alone, or one of the grey hens if you prefer, for that is a thing that will never be known, though it might well have been, without much trouble. For all that was necessary, in order that it might be known whether there was only one grey hen or more than one, was for someone to be present when all the hens came running towards Mrs. Lambert as she cried, Tweet! Tweet!, and banged on an old tin with an old spoon. But after all what use would that have been? For it was quite possible there were several grey hens, and yet only one in the habit of coming to the kitchen. And yet the experiment was worth making. For it was quite possible there was only one grey hen, even at feeding-time. Which would have clinched the matter. And yet that is a thing that will never be known. For among those who must have known, some are dead and the others have forgotten. And the day when it was urgent for Sapo to have this point cleared up, and his mind set at rest, it was too late. Then he was sorry he had not understood, in time to profit by it, the importance that those hours were one day to assume, for him, those long hours in that old kitchen where, neither quite indoors nor quite out of doors, he waited to be on his feet again, and in motion, and while waiting noted many things, among them this big, anxious, ashen bird, poised irresolute on the bright threshold, then clucking and clawing behind the range and fidgeting her atrophied wings, soon to be sent flying with a broom and angry cries and soon to return, cautiously, with little hesitant steps, stopping often to listen, opening and shutting her little bright black eyes. And so he went, all unsuspecting, with the fond impression of having been present at everyday scenes of no import. He stooped to cross the threshold and saw before him the well, with its winch, chain and bucket, and often too a long line of tattered washing, swaying and drying in the sun. He went by the little path he had come by, along the edge of the meadow in the shadow of the great trees that bordered the stream, its bed a chaos of gnarled roots, boulders and baked mud. And so he went, often unnoticed, in spite of his strange walk, his halts and sudden starts. Or the Lamberts saw him, from far off or from near by, or some of them from far off and the others from near by, suddenly emerge from behind the washing and set off down the path. Then they did not try to detain him or even call goodbye, unresentful at his leaving them in a way that seemed so lacking in friendliness, for they knew he meant no harm. Or if at the time they could not help feeling a little hurt, this feeling was quite dispelled a little later, when they found on the kitchen-table the crumpled paper-bag containing a few little articles of haberdashery. And these humble presents, but oh how useful, and this oh so delicate way of giving, disarmed them too at the sight of the bowl of goat's milk only half emptied, or left untouched, and prevented them from regarding this as an affront, in the way tradition required. But it would appear on reflection that Sapo's departure can seldom have escaped them. For at the least moment within sight of their land, were it only that of a little bird alighting or taking to wing, they raised their heads and stared with wide eyes. And even on the road, of which segments were visible more than a mile away, nothing could happen without their knowledge, and they were able not only to identify all those who passed along it and whose remoteness reduced them to the size of a pin's head, but also to divine whence they were coming, where they were going, and for what purpose. Then they cried the news to one another, for they often worked at a great distance apart, or they exchanged signals, all erect and turned towards the event, for it was one, before bowing themselves down to the earth again. And at the first spell of rest taken in common, about the table or elsewhere, each one gave his version of what had passed and listened to those of the others. And if at first they were not in agreement about what they had seen, they talked it over doggedly until they were, in agreement I mean, or until they resigned themselves to never being so. It was therefore difficult for Sapo to glide away unseen, even in the deep shadow of the trees that bordered the stream, even supposing him to have been capable of gliding, for his movements were rather those of one floundering in a quag. And all raised their heads and watched him as he went, then looked at one another, before stooping to the earth again. And on each face bent to the earth there played perhaps a little smile, a little rictus rather, but without malice, each wondering perhaps if the others felt the same thing and making the resolve to ask them, at their next meeting. But the face of Sapo as he stumbled away, now in the shadow of the venerable trees he could not name, now in the brightness of the waving meadow, so erratic was his course, the face of Sapo was as always grave, or rather expressionless. And when he halted it was not the better to think, or the closer to pore upon his dream, but simply because the voice had ceased that told him to go on. Then with his pale eyes he stared down at the earth, blind to its beauty, and to its utility, and to the little wild many-coloured flowers happy among the crops and weeds. But these stations were short-lived, for he was still young. And of a sudden he is off again, on his wanderings, passing from light to shadow, from shadow to light, unheedingly.

When I stop, as just now, the noises begin again, strangely loud, those whose turn it is. So that I seem to have again the hearing of my boyhood. Then in my bed, in the dark, on stormy nights, I could tell from one another, in the outcry without, the leaves, the boughs, the groaning trunks, even the grasses and the house that sheltered me. Each tree had its own cry, just as no two whispered alike, when the air was still. I heard afar the iron gates clashing and dragging at their posts and the wind rushing between their bars. There was nothing, not even the sand on the paths, that did not utter its cry. The still nights too, still as the grave as the saying is, were nights of storm for me, clamorous with countless pantings. These I amused myself with identifying, as I lay there. Yes, I got great amusement, when young, from their so-called silence. The sound I liked best had nothing noble about it. It was the barking of the dogs, at night, in the clusters of hovels up in the hills, where the stone-cutters lived, like generations of stone-cutters before them. It came down to me where I lay, in the house in the plain, wild and soft, at the limit of earshot, soon weary. The dogs of the valley replied with their gross bay all fangs and jaws and foam. From the hills another joy came down, I mean the brief scattered lights that sprang up on their slopes at nightfall, merging in blurs scarcely brighter than the sky, less bright than the stars, and which the palest moon extinguished. They were things that scarcely were, on the confines of silence and dark, and soon ceased. So I reason now, at my ease. Standing before my high window I gave myself to them, waiting for them to end, for my joy to end, straining towards the joy of ended joy. But our business at the moment is less with these futilities than with my ears from which there spring two impetuous tufts of no doubt yellow hair, yellowed by wax and lack of care, and so long that the lobes are hidden. I note then, without emotion, that of late their hearing seems to have improved. Oh not that I was ever even incompletely deaf. But for a long time now I have been hearing things confusedly. There I go again. What I mean is possibly this, that the noises of the world, so various in themselves and which I used to be so clever at distinguishing from one another, had been dinning at me for so long, always the same old noises, as gradually to have merged into a single noise, so that all I heard was one vast continuous buzzing. The volume of sound perceived remained no doubt the same, I had simply lost the faculty of decomposing it. The noises of nature, of mankind and even my own, were all jumbled together in one and the same unbridled gibberish. Enough. I would willingly attribute part of my shall I say my misfortunes to this disordered sense were I not unfortunately rather inclined to look upon it as a blessing. Misfortunes, blessings, I have no time to pick my words, I am in a hurry to be done. And yet no, I am in no hurry. Decidedly this evening I shall say nothing that is not false, I mean nothing that is not calculated to leave me in doubt as to my real intentions. For it is evening, even night, one of the darkest I can remember, I have a short memory. My little finger glides before my pencil across the page and gives warning, falling over the edge, that the end of the line is near. But in the other direction, I mean of course vertically, I have nothing to guide me. I did not want to write, but I had to resign myself to it in the end. It is in order to know where I have got to, where he has got to. At first I did not write, I just said the thing. Then I forgot what I had said. A minimum of memory is indispensable, if one is to live really. Take his family, for example, I really know practically nothing about his family any more. But that does not worry me, there is a record of it somewhere. It is the only way to keep an eye on him. But as far as I myself am concerned the same necessity does not arise, or does it? And yet I write about myself with the same pencil and in the same exercise-book as about him. It is because it is no longer I, I must have said so long ago, but another whose life is just beginning. It is right that he too should have his little chronicle, his memories, his reason, and be able to recognize the good in the bad, the bad in the worst, and so grow gently old all down the unchanging days and die one day like any other day, only shorter. That is my excuse. But there must be others, no less excellent. Yes, it is quite dark. I can see nothing. I can scarcely even see the window-pane, or the wall forming with it so sharp a contrast that it often looks like the edge of an abyss. I hear the noise of my little finger as it glides over the paper and then that so different of the pencil following after. That is what surprises me and makes me say that something must have changed. Whence that child I might have been, why not? And I hear also, there we are at last, I hear a choir, far enough away for me not to hear it when it goes soft. It is a song I know, I don't know how, and when it fades, and when it dies quite away, it goes on inside me, but too slow, or too fast, for when it comes on the air to me again it is not together with mine, but behind, or ahead. It is a mixed choir, or I am greatly deceived. With children too perhaps. I have the absurd feeling it is conducted by a woman. It has been singing the same song for a long time now. They must be rehearsing. It belongs already to the long past, it has uttered for the last time the triumphal cry on which it ends. Can it be Easter Week? Thus with the year Seasons return. If it can, could not this song I have just heard, and which quite frankly is not yet quite stilled within me, could not this song have simply been to the honour and glory of him who was the first to rise from the dead, to him who saved me, twenty centuries in advance? Did I say the first? The final bawl lends colour to this view.

I fear I must have fallen asleep again. In vain I grope, I cannot find my exercise-book. But I still have the pencil in my hand. I shall have to wait for day to break. God knows what I am going to do till then.

I have just written, I fear I must have fallen, etc. I hope this is not too great a distortion of the truth. I now add these few lines, before departing from myself again. I do not depart from myself now with the same avidity as a week ago for example. For this must be going on now for over a week, it must be over a week since I said, I shall soon be quite dead at last, etc. Wrong again. That is not what I said, I could swear to it, that is what I wrote. This last phrase seems familiar, suddenly I seem to have written it somewhere before, or spoken it, word for word.

Yes, I shall soon be, etc., that is what I wrote when I realized I did not know what I had said, at the beginning of my say, and subsequently, and that consequently the plan I had formed, to live, and cause to live, at last, to play at last and die alive, was going the way of all my other plans. I think the dawn was not so slow in coming as I had feared, I really do. But I feared nothing, I fear nothing any more. High summer is truly at hand. Turned towards the window I saw the pane shiver at last, before the ghastly sunrise. It is no ordinary pane, it brings me sunset and it brings me sunrise. The exercise-book had fallen to the ground. I took a long time to find it. It was under the bed. How are such things possible? I took a long time to recover it. I had to harpoon it. It is not pierced through and through, but it is in a bad way. It is a thick exercise-book. I hope it will see me out. From now on I shall write on both sides of the page. Where does it come from? I don't know. I found it, just like that, the day I needed it. Knowing perfectly well I had no exercise-book I rummaged in my possessions in the hope of finding one. I was not disappointed, not surprised. If to-morrow I needed an old love-letter I would adopt the same method. It is ruled in squares. The first pages are covered with ciphers and other symbols and diagrams, with here and there a brief phrase. Calculations, I reckon. They seem to stop suddenly, prematurely at all events. As though discouraged. Perhaps it is astronomy, or astrology. I did not look closely. I drew a line, no, I did not even draw a line, and I wrote, Soon I shall be quite dead at last, and so on, without even going on to the next page, which was blank. Good. Now I need not dilate on this exercise-book when it comes to the inventory, but merely say, Item, an exercise-book, giving perhaps the colour of the cover. But I may well lose it between now and then, for good and all. The pencil on the contrary is an old acquaintance, I must have had it about me when I was brought here. It has five faces. It is very short. It is pointed at both ends. A Venus. I hope it will see me out. I was saying I did not depart from myself now with quite the same alacrity. That must be in the natural order of things, all that pertains to me must be written there, including my inability to grasp what order is meant. For I have never seen any sign of any, inside me or outside me. I have pinned my faith to appearances, believing them to be vain. I shall not go into the details. Choke, go down, come up, choke, suppose, deny, affirm, drown. I depart from myself less gladly. Amen. I waited for the dawn. Doing what? I don't know. What I had to do. I watched for the window. I gave rein to my pains, my impotence. And in the end it seemed to me, for a second, that I was going to have a visit!

The summer holidays were drawing to a close. The decisive moment was at hand when the hopes reposed in Sapo were to be fulfilled, or dashed to the ground. He is trained to a hair, said Mr. Saposcat. And Mrs. Saposcat, whose piety grew warm in times of crisis, prayed for his success. Kneeling at her bedside, in her night-dress, she ejaculated, silently, for her husband would not have approved, Oh God grant he pass, grant he pass, grant he scrape through!

When this first ordeal was surmounted there would be others, every year, several times a year. But it seemed to the Saposcats that these would be less terrible than the first which was to give them, or deny them, the right to say, He is doing his medicine, or, He is reading for the bar. For they felt that a more or less normal if unintelligent youth, once admitted to the study of these professions, was almost sure to be certified, sooner or later, apt to exercise them. For they had experience of doctors, and of lawyers, like most people.

One day Mr. Saposcat sold himself a fountain-pen, at a discount. A Bird. I shall give it to him on the morning of the examination, he said. He took off the long cardboard lid and showed the pen to his wife. Leave it in its box! he cried, as she made to take it in her hand. It lay almost hidden in the scrolled leaflet containing the instructions for use. Mr. Saposcat parted the edges of the paper and held up the box for his wife to look inside. But she, instead of looking at the pen, looked at him.

He named the price. Might it not be better, she said, to let him have it the day before, to give him time to get used to the nib? You are right, he said, I had not thought of that. Or even two days before, she said, to give him time to change the nib if it does not suit him. A bird, its yellow beak agape to show it was singing, adorned the lid, which Mr. Saposcat now put on again. He wrapped with expert hands the box in tissue-paper and slipped over it a narrow rubber band. He was not pleased. It is a medium nib, he said, and it will certainly suit him.

This conversation was renewed the next day. Mr. Saposcat said, Might it not be better if we just lent him the pen and told him he could keep it for his own, if he passed? Then we must do so at once, said Mrs. Saposcat, otherwise there is no point in it. To which Mr. Saposcat made, after a silence, a first objection, and then, after a second silence, a second objection. He first objected that his son, if he received the pen forthwith, would have time to break it, or lose it, before the paper. He secondly objected that his son, if he received the pen immediately, and assuming he neither broke nor lost it, would have time to get so used to it and, by comparing it with the pens of his less impoverished friends, so familiar with its defects, that its possession would no longer tempt him. I did not know it was an inferior article, said Mrs. Saposcat. Mr. Saposcat placed his hand on the table-cloth and sat gazing at it for some time. Then he laid down his napkin and left the room. Adrian, cried Mrs. Saposcat, come back and finish your sweet! Alone before the table she listened to the steps on the garden-path, clearer, fainter, clearer, fainter.

The Lamberts. One day Sapo arrived at the farm earlier than usual. But do we know what time he usually arrived? Lengthening, fading shadows. He was surprised to see, at a distance, in the midst of the young stubble, the father's big red and white head. His body was in the hole or pit he had dug for his mule, which had died during the night. Edmund came out of the house, wiping his mouth, and joined him. Lambert then climbed out of

the hole and the son went down into it. Drawing closer Sapo
saw the mule's black corpse. Then all became clear to him. The
mule was lying on its side, as was to be expected. The forelegs
were stretched out straight and rigid, the hind drawn up under the
belly. The yawning jaws, the wreathed lips, the enormous teeth,
the bulging eyes, composed a striking death's-head. Edmund
handed up to his father the pick, the shovel and the spade and
climbed out of the hole. Together they dragged the mule by
the legs to the edge of the hole and heaved it in, on its back.
The forelegs, pointing towards heaven, projected above the level
of the ground. Old Lambert banged them down with his spade.
He handed the spade to his son and went towards the house.
Edmund began to fill up the hole. Sapo stood watching him.
A great calm stole over him. Great calm is an exaggeration. He
felt better. The end of a life is always vivifying. Edmund paused
to rest, leaned panting on the spade and smiled. There were
great pink gaps in his front teeth. Big Lambert sat by the window, smoking, drinking, watching his son. Sapo sat down
before him, laid his hand on the table and his head on his
hand, thinking he was alone. Between his head and his hand he
slipped the other hand and sat there marble still. Louis began
to talk. He seemed in good spirits. The mule, in his opinion,
had died of old age. He had bought it, two years before, on
its way to the slaughter-house. So he could not complain. After
the transaction the owner of the mule predicted that it would drop
down dead at the first ploughing. But Lambert was a connoisseur
of mules. In the case of mules it is the eye that counts, the
rest is unimportant. So he looked the mule full in the eye, at
the gates of the slaughter-house, and saw it could still be made
to serve. And the mule returned his gaze, in the yard of the
slaughter-house. As Lambert unfolded his story the slaughter-
house loomed larger and larger. Thus the site of the transaction
shifted gradually from the road that led to the slaughter-house
to the gates of the slaughter-house and thence to the yard itself.
Yet a little while and he would have contended for the mule with

the knacker. The look in his eye, he said, was like a prayer to
me to take him. It was covered with sores, but in the case of
mules one should never let oneself be deterred by senile sores.
Someone said, He's done ten miles already, you'll never get him
home, he'll drop down dead on the road. I thought I might
screw six months out of him, said Lambert, and I screwed two
years. All the time he told this story he kept his eyes fixed on
his son. There they sat, the table between them, in the gloom, one
speaking, the other listening, and far removed, the one from
what he said, the other from what he heard, and far from each
other. The heap of earth was dwindling, the earth shone
strangely in the raking evening light, glowing in patches as
though with its own fires, in the fading light. Edmund stopped
often to rest, leaning on the spade and looking about him. The
slaughter-house, said Lambert, that's where I buy my beasts, will
you look at that loafer. He went out and set to work, beside his
son. They worked together for a time, heedless of each other.
Then the son dropped his shovel, turned aside and moved slowly
away, passing from toil to rest in a single unbroken movement
that did not seem of his doing. The mule was no longer visible.
The face of the earth, on which it had plodded its life away,
would see it no more, toiling before the plough, or the dray.
And Big Lambert would soon be able to plough and harrow the
place where it lay, with another mule, or an old horse, or an old
ox, bought at the knacker's yard, knowing that the share would
not turn up the putrid flesh or be blunted by the big bones. For
he knew how the dead and buried tend, contrary to what one
might expect, to rise to the surface, in which they resemble the
drowned. And he had made allowance for this when digging the
hole. Edmund and his mother passed each other by in silence. She
had been to see a neighbour, to borrow a pound of lentils for
their supper. She was thinking of the handsome steelyard that
had served to weigh them and wondering if it was true. Before
her husband too she rapidly passed, without a glance, and in his
attitude there was nothing to suggest that he had seen her either.
She lit the lamp where it stood at its usual place on the chimney-

piece, beside the alarm-clock flanked in its turn by a crucifix hanging from a nail. The clock, being the lowest of the three, had to remain in the middle, and the lamp and crucifix could not change places because of the nail from which the latter was hung. She stood with her forehead and her hands pressed against the wall, until she might turn up the wick. She turned it up and put on the yellow globe which a large hole defaced. Seeing Sapo she first thought he was her daughter. Then her thoughts flew to the absent one. She set down the lamp on the table and the outer world went out. She sat down, emptied out the lentils on the table and began to sort them. So that soon there were two heaps on the table, one big heap getting smaller and one small heap getting bigger. But suddenly with a furious gesture she swept the two together, annihilating thus in less than a second the work of two or three minutes. Then she went away and came back with a saucepan. It won't kill them, she said, and with the heel of her hand she brought the lentils to the edge of the table and over the edge into the saucepan, as if all that mattered was not to be killed, but so clumsily and with such nervous haste that a great number fell wide of the pan to the ground. Then she took up the lamp and went out, to fetch wood perhaps, or a lump of fat bacon. Now that it was dark again in the kitchen the dark outside gradually lightened and Sapo, his eye against the window-pane, was able to discern certain shapes, including that of Big Lambert stamping the ground. To stop in the middle of a tedious and perhaps futile task was something that Sapo could readily understand. For a great number of tasks are of this kind, without a doubt, and the only way to end them is to abandon them. She could have gone on sorting her lentils all night and never achieved her purpose, which was to free them from all admixture. But in the end she would have stopped, saying, I have done all I can do. But she would not have done all she could have done. But the moment comes when one desists, because it is the wisest thing to do, discouraged, but not to the extent of undoing all that has been done. But what if her purpose, in sorting the lentils, were not to rid them of all that was not lentil, but only of the greater part, what then? I don't know. Whereas there are other tasks, other days, of which one may fairly safely say that they are finished, though I do not see which. She came back, holding the lamp high and a little to one side, so as not to be dazzled. In the other hand she held a white rabbit, by the hindlegs. For whereas the mule had been black, the rabbit had been white. It was dead already, it had ceased to be. There are rabbits that die before they are killed, from sheer fright. They have time to do so while being taken out of the hutch, often by the ears, and disposed in the most convenient position to receive the blow, whether on the back of the neck or on some other part. And often you strike a corpse, without knowing it. For you have just seen the rabbit alive and well behind the wire meshing, nibbling at its leaves. And you congratulate yourself on having succeeded with the first blow, and not caused unnecessary suffering, whereas in reality you have taken all that trouble for nothing. This occurs most frequently at night, fright being greater in the night. Hens on the other hand are more stubborn livers and some have been observed, with the head already off, to cut a few last capers before collapsing. Pigeons too are less impressionable and sometimes even struggle, before choking to death. Mrs. Lambert was breathing hard. Little devil! she cried. But Sapo was already far away, trailing his hand in the high waving meadow grasses. Soon afterwards Lambert, then his son, attracted by the savoury smell, entered the kitchen. Sitting at the table, face to face, their eyes averted from each other's eyes, they waited. But the woman, the mother, went to the door and called. Lizzy! she cried, again and again. Then she went back to her range. She had seen the moon. After a silence Lambert declared, I'll kill Whitey tomorrow. Those of course were not the words he used, but that was the meaning. But neither his wife nor his son could approve him, the former because she would have preferred him to kill Blackey, the latter because he held that to kill the kids at such an early stage of their development, either of them, it was all the same to him, would be premature. But Big Lambert told them to hold their tongues and went to the corner to fetch the

40

case containing the knives, three in number. All he had to do was to wipe off the grease and whet them a little on one another. Mrs. Lambert went back to the door, listened, called. In the far distance the flock replied. She's coming, she said. But a long time passed before she came. When the meal was over Edmund went up to bed, so as to masturbate in peace and comfort before his sister joined him, for they shared the same room. Not that he was restrained by modesty, when his sister was there. Nor was she, when her brother was there. Their quarters were cramped, certain refinements were not possible. Edmund then went up to bed, for no particular reason. He would have gladly slept with his sister, the father too, I mean the father would have gladly slept with his daughter, the time was long past and gone when he would have gladly slept with his sister. But something held them back. And she did not seem eager. But she was still young. Incest then was in the air. Mrs. Lambert, the only member of the household who had no desire to sleep with anybody, saw it coming with indifference. She went out. Alone with his daughter Lambert sat watching her. She was crouched before the range, in an attitude of dejection. He told her to eat and she began to eat the remains of the rabbit, out of the pot, with a spoon. But it is hard to look steadily for any length of time at a fellow-creature, even when you are resolved to, and suddenly Lambert saw his daughter at another place and otherwise engaged than in bringing the spoon up from the pot into her mouth and down from her mouth into the pot again. And yet he could have sworn that he had not taken his eyes off her. He said, To-morrow we'll kill Whitey, you can hold her if you like. But seeing her still so sad, and her cheeks wet with tears, he went towards her.

What tedium. If I went on to the stone? No, it would be the same thing. The Lamberts, the Lamberts, does it matter about the Lamberts? No, not particularly. But while I am with them the other is lost. How are my plans getting on, my plans, I had plans not so long ago. Perhaps I have another ten years ahead

41

of me. The Lamberts! I shall try and go on all the same, a little longer, my thoughts elsewhere, I can't stay here. I shall hear myself talking, afar off, from my far mind, talking of the Lamberts, talking of myself, my mind wandering, far from here, among its ruins.

Then Mrs. Lambert was alone in the kitchen. She sat down by the window and turned down the wick of the lamp, as she always did before blowing it out, for she did not like to blow out a lamp that was still hot. When she thought the chimney and shade had cooled sufficiently she got up and blew down the chimney. She stood a moment irresolute, bowed forward with her hands on the table, before she sat down again. Her day of toil over, day dawned on other toils within her, on the crass tenacity of life and its diligent pains. Sitting, moving about, she bore them better than in bed. From the well of this unending weariness her sigh went up unendingly, for day when it was night, for night when it was day, and day and night, fearfully, for the light she had been told about, and told she could never understand, because it was not like those she knew, not like the summer dawn she knew would come again, to her waiting in the kitchen, sitting up straight on the chair, or bowed down over the table, with little sleep, little rest, but more than in her bed. Often she stood up and moved about the room, or out and round the ruinous old house. Five years now it had been going on, five or six, not more. She told herself she had a woman's disease, but half-heartedly. Night seemed less night in the kitchen pervaded with the everyday tribulations, day less dead. It helped her, when things were bad, to cling with her fingers to the worn table at which her family would soon be united, waiting for her to serve them, and to feel about her, ready for use, the lifelong pots and pans. She opened the door and looked out. The moon had gone, but the stars were shining. She stood gazing up at them. It was a scene that had sometimes solaced her. She went to the well and grasped the chain. The bucket was at the bottom, the windlass locked. So it was. Her fingers strayed along the sinuous links. Her mind was a press of formless questions, mingling and crumbling limply away. Some seemed to have to do with her daughter, that minor worry, now lying sleepless in her bed, listening. Hearing her mother moving about, she was on the point of getting up and going down to her. But it was only the next day, or the day after, that she decided to tell her what Sapo had told her, namely that he was going away and would not come back. Then, as people do when someone even insignificant dies, they summoned up such memories as he had left them, helping one another and trying to agree. But we all know that little flame and its flickerings in the wild shadows. And agreement only comes a little later, with the forgetting.

Mortal tedium. One day I took counsel of an Israelite on the subject of conation. That must have been when I was still looking for someone to be faithful to me, and for me to be faithful to. Then I opened wide my eyes so that the candidates might admire their bottomless depths and the way they phosphoresced at all we left unspoken. Our faces were so close that I felt on mine the wafts of hot air and sprays of saliva, and he too, no doubt, on his. I can see him still, the fit of laughter past, wiping his eyes and mouth, and myself, with downcast eyes, pained by my wetted trousers and the little pool of urine at my feet. Now that I have no further use for him I may as well give his name, Jackson. I was sorry he had not a cat, or a young dog, or better still an old dog. But all he had to offer in the way of dumb companions was a pink and grey parrot. He used to try and teach it to say, Nihil in intellectu, etc. These first three words the bird managed well enough, but the celebrated restriction was too much for it, all you heard was a series of squawks. This annoyed Jackson, who kept nagging at it to begin all over again. Then Polly flew into a rage and retreated to a corner of its cage. It was a very fine cage, with every convenience, perches, swings, trays, troughs, stairs and cuttle-bones. It was even overcrowed, personally I would have felt cramped. Jackson called me the merino, I don't know why, perhaps because of the French expression. I could not help thinking that the notion of a wandering herd was better adapted to him than to me. But I have never thought anything but wind, the same that was never measured to me. My relations with Jackson were of short duration. I could have put up with him as a friend, but unfortunately he found me disgusting, as did Johnson, Wilson, Nicholson and Watson, all whoresons. I then tried, for a space, to lay hold of a kindred spirit among the inferior races, red, yellow, chocolate, and so on. And if the plague-stricken had been less difficult of access I would have intruded on them too, ogling, sidling, leering, ineffing and conating, my heart palpitating. With the insane too I failed, by a hair's-breadth. That must have been the way with me then. But the point is rather what is the way with me now. When young the old filled me with wonder and awe. Bawling babies are what dumbfound me now. The house is full of them finally. Suave mari magno, especially for the old salt. What tedium. And I thought I had it all thought out. If I had the use of my body I would throw it out of the window. But perhaps it is the knowledge of my impotence that emboldens me to that thought. All hangs together, I am in chains. Unfortunately I do not know quite what floor I am on, perhaps I am only on the mezzanine. The doors banging, the steps on the stairs, the noises in the street, have not enlightened me, on this subject. All I know is that the living are there, above me and beneath me. It follows at least that I am not in the basement. And do I not sometimes see the sky and sometimes, through my window, other windows facing it apparently? But that proves nothing, I do not wish to prove anything. Or so I say. Perhaps after all I am in a kind of vault and this space which I take to be the street in reality no more than a wide trench or ditch with other vaults opening upon it. But the noises that rise up from below, the steps that come climbing towards me? Perhaps there are other vaults even deeper than mine, why not? In which case the question arises again as to which floor I am on, there is nothing to be gained by my saying I am in a basement if there are tiers of basements one on top of another. But the noises that I say rise up from below, the steps that I say come climbing towards me, do they really do so? I have no proof that they do. To conclude from this that I am a prey to hallucinations pure and simple is however a step I hesitate to take. And I honestly believe that in this house there are people coming and going and even conversing, and multitudes of fine babies, particularly of late, which the parents keep moving about from one place to another, to prevent their forming the habit of motionlessness, in anticipation of the day when they will have to move about unaided. But all things considered I would be hard set to say for certain where exactly they are, in relation to where exactly I am. And when all is said and done there is nothing more like a step that climbs than a step that descends or even that paces to and fro forever on the same level, I mean for one not only in ignorance of his position and consequently of what he is to expect, in the way of sounds, but at the same time more than half-deaf more than half the time. There is naturally another possibility that does not escape me, though it would be a great disappointment to have it confirmed, and that is that I am dead already and that all continues more or less as when I was not. Perhaps I expired in the forest, or even earlier. In which case all the trouble I have been taking for some time past, for what purpose I do not clearly recall except that it was in some way connected with the feeling that my troubles were nearly over, has been to no purpose whatsoever. But my horse-sense tells me I have not yet quite ceased to gasp. And it summons in support of this view various considerations having to do for example with the little heap of my possessions, my system of nutrition and elimination, the couple across the way, the changing sky, and so on. Whereas in reality all that is perhaps nothing but my worms. Take for example the light that reigns in this den and of which the least that can be said, really the least, is that it is bizarre. I enjoy a kind of night and day, admittedly, often it is even pitch dark, but in rather a different way from the way to which I fancy I was accustomed, before I found myself here. Example, there is nothing like examples, I was once in utter darkness and waiting with some impatience for dawn to break, having need of its light to see to certain little things which it is difficult to see to in the dark. And sure enough little by little the dark lightened and I was able to hook with my stick the objects I required. But the light, instead of being the dawn, turned out in a very short time to be the dusk. And the sun, instead of rising higher and higher in the sky as I confidently expected, calmly set, and night, the passing of which I had just celebrated after my fashion, calmly fell again. Now the reverse, as you might say, I mean day closing in the twi-light of dawn, I must confess to never having experienced, and that goes to my heart, I mean that I cannot bring myself to declare that I experienced that too. And yet how often I have implored night to fall, all the livelong day, with all my feeble strength, and how often day to break, all the livelong night. But before leaving this subject and entering upon another, I feel it is my duty to say that it is never light in this place, never really light. The light is there, outside, the air sparkles, the granite wall across the way glitters with all its mica, the light is against my window, but it does not come through. So that here all bathes, I will not say in shadow, nor even in half-shadow, but in a kind of leaden light that makes no shadow, so that it is hard to say from what direction it comes, for it seems to come from all directions at once, and with equal force. I am convinced for example that at the present moment it is as bright under my bed as it is under the ceiling, which ad-mittedly is not saying much, but I need say no more. And does not that amount to simply this, that there is really no color in this place, except in so far as this kind of grey incandescence may be called a color? Yes, no doubt one may speak of grey, personally I have no objection, in which case the issue here would lie between this grey and the black that it overlays more or less, I was going to say according to the time of day, but no, it does not always seem to depend on the time of day. I myself am very grey, I even sometimes have the feeling that I emit grey, in the same way as my sheets for example. And my night is not the sky's. Naturally black is black the whole world over. But how is it my little space is not visited by the luminaries I sometimes see shining afar and how is it the moon where Cain toils bowed beneath his burden never sheds its light on my face? In a word there seems to be the light of the outer world, of those who know the sun and moon emerge at such an hour and at such another plunge again below the surface, and who rely on this, and who know that clouds are always to be expected but sooner or later always pass away, and mine. But mine too has its alternations, I will not deny it, its dusks and dawns, but that is what I say, for I too must have lived, once, out there, and there is no recovering from that. And when I examine the ceiling and walls I see there is no possibility of my making light, artificial light, like the couple across the way for example. But someone would have to give me a lamp, or a torch, you know, and I don't know if the air here is of the kind that lends itself to the comedy of combustion. Mem, look for a match in my possessions, and see if it burns. The noises too, cries, steps, doors, murmurs, cease for whole days, their days. Than that silence of which, knowing what I know, I shall merely say that there is nothing, how shall I merely say, nothing negative about it. And softly my little space begins to throb again. You may say it is all in my head, and indeed sometimes it seems to me I am in a head and that these eight, no, six, these six planes that enclose me are of solid bone. But thence to conclude the head is mine, no, never. A kind of air circulates, I must have said so, and when all goes still I hear it beating against the walls and being beaten back by them. And then somewhere in midspace other waves, other onslaughts, gather and break, whence I suppose the faint sound of aerial surf that is my silence. Or else it is the sudden storm, analogous to those outside, rising and drowning the cries of the children, the dying, the lovers, so that in my innocence I say they cease, whereas in reality they never cease. It is difficult to decide. And in the skull is it a vacuum? I ask. And if I close my eyes, close them really, as others cannot, but

47

as I can, for there are limits to my impotence, then sometimes my bed is caught up into the air and tossed like a straw by the swirling eddies, and I in it. Fortunately it is not so much an affair of eyelids, but as it were the soul that must be veiled, that soul denied in vain, vigilant, anxious, turning in its cage as in a lantern, in the night without haven or craft or matter or understanding. Ah yes, I have my little pastimes and they

What a misfortune, the pencil must have slipped from my fingers, for I have only just succeeded in recovering it after forty-eight hours (see above) of intermittent efforts. What my stick lacks is a little prehensile proboscis like the nocturnal tapir's. I should really lose my pencil more often, it might do me good, I might be more cheerful, it might be more cheerful. I have spent two unforgettable days of which nothing will ever be known, it is too late now, or still too soon, I forget which, except that they have brought me the solution and conclusion of the whole sorry business, I mean the business of Malone (since that is what I am called now) and of the other, for the rest is no business of mine. And it was, though more unutterable, like the crumbling away of two little heaps of finest sand, or dust, or ashes, of unequal size, but diminishing together as it were in ratio, if that means anything, and leaving behind them, each in its own stead, the blessedness of absence. While this was going on I was struggling to retrieve my pencil, by fits and starts. My pencil. It is a little Venus, still green no doubt, with five or six facets, pointed at both ends and so short there is just room, between them, for my thumb and the two adjacent fingers, gathered together in a little vice. I use the two points turn and turn about, sucking them frequently, I love to suck. And when they go quite blunt I strip them with my nails which are long, yellow, sharp and brittle for want of chalk or is it phosphate. So little by little my little pencil dwindles, inevitably, and the day is fast approaching when nothing will remain but a fragment too tiny to hold. So I write as lightly as I can. But the lead is hard and would leave no trace if I wrote too lightly. But I say to myself, Between a hard lead with which one dare not write too lightly, if a trace is to be left, and a soft fat lead which blackens the page almost without touching it, what possible difference can there be, from the point of view of durability. Ah yes, I have my little pastimes. The strange thing is I have another pencil, made in France, a long cylinder hardly broached, in the bed with me somewhere I think. So I have nothing to worry about, on this score. And yet I do worry. Now while I was hunting for my pencil I made a curious discovery. The floor is whitening. I struck it several blows with my stick and the sound it gave forth was at once sharp and dull, wrong in fact. So it was not without some trepidation that I inspected the other great planes, above and all about me. And all this time the sand kept trickling away and I saying to myself, It is gone for ever, meaning of course the pencil. And I saw that all these superficies, or should I say infraficies, the horizontal as well as the perpendicular, though they do not look particularly perpendicular from here, had visibly blanched since my last examination of them, dating from I know not when. And this is all the more singular as the tendency of things in general is I believe rather to darken, as time wears on, with of course the exception of our mortal remains and certain parts of the body which lose their natural color and from which the blood recedes in the long run. Does this mean there is more light here now, now that I know what is going on? No, I fear not, it is the same grey as heretofore, literally sparkling at times, then growing murky and dim, thickening is perhaps the word, until all things are blotted out except the window which seems in a manner of speaking to be my umbilicus, so that I say to myself, When it too goes out I shall know more or less where I am. No, all I mean is this, that when I open staring wide my eyes I see at the confines of this restless gloom a gleaming and shimmering as of bones, which was not hitherto the case, to the best of my knowledge. And I can even distinctly remember the paper-hangings or wall-paper still clinging in places to the walls and covered with a writing mass of roses, violets and other flowers in such profusion that it seemed to me I had never seen so many in the whole course of my life, nor of such beauty. But now they seem to be all gone, quite gone, and if there were no flowers on the ceiling there was no doubt something else, cupids perhaps, gone too, without leaving a trace. And while I was busy pursuing my pencil a moment came when my exercise-book, almost a child's, fell also to the ground. But it I very soon recovered, slipping the hook of my stick into one of the rents in the cover and hoisting it gently towards me. And during all this time, so fertile in incidents and mishaps, in my head I suppose all was streaming and emptying away as through a sluice, to my great joy, until finally nothing remained, either of Malone or of the other. And what is more I was able to follow without difficulty the various phases of this deliverance and felt no surprise at its irregular course, now rapid, now slow, so crystal clear was my understanding of the reasons why this could not be otherwise. And I rejoiced furthermore, quite apart from the spectacle, at the thought that I now knew what I had to do, I whose every move has always been a groping, and whose motionlessness too was a kind of groping, yes, I have greatly groped stockstill. And here again naturally I was utterly deceived, I mean in imagining I had grasped at last the true nature of my absurd tribulations, but not so utterly as to feel the need to reproach myself with it now. For even as I said, How easy and beautiful it all is!, in the same breath I said, All will grow dark again. And it is without excessive sorrow that I see us again as we are, namely to be removed grain by grain until the hand, wearied, begins to play, scooping us up and letting us trickle back into the same place, dreamily as the saying is. For I knew it would be so, even as I said, At last! And I must say that to me at least and for as long as I can remember the sensation is familiar of a blind and tired hand delving feebly in my particles and letting them trickle between its fingers. And sometimes, when all is quiet, I feel it plunged in me up to the elbow, but gentle, and as though sleeping. But soon it stirs, wakes, fondles, clutches, ransacks, ravages, avenging its failure to scatter me with one sweep. I can understand. But I have felt so many strange things, so many baseless things assuredly, that they are perhaps better left unsaid. To speak for example of the times when I go liquid and become like mud, what good would that do? Or of the others when I would be lost in the eye of a needle, I am so hard and contracted? No, those are well-meaning squirms that get me nowhere. I was speaking then was I not of my little pastimes and I think about to say that I ought to content myself with them, instead of launching forth on all this ballsaching poppycock about life and death, if that is what it is all about, and I suppose it is, for nothing was ever about anything else to the best of my recollection. But what it is all about exactly I could no more say, at the present moment, than take up my bed and walk. It's vague, life and death. I must have had my little private idea on the subject when I began, otherwise I would not have begun, I would have held my peace, I would have gone on peacefully being bored to howls, having my little fun and games with the cones and cylinders, the millet grains beloved of birds and other panics, until someone was kind enough to come and coffin me. But it is gone clean out of my head, my little private idea. No matter, I have just had another. Perhaps it is the same one back again, ideas are so alike, when you get to know them. Be born, that's the brainwave now, that is to say live long enough to get acquainted with free carbonic gas, then say thanks for the nice time and go. That has always been my dream at bottom, all the things that have always been my dream at bottom, so many strings and never a shaft. Yes, an old foetus, that's what I am now, hoar and impotent, mother is done for, I've rotted her, she'll drop me with the help of gangrene, perhaps papa is at the party too, I'll land head-foremost mewling in the charnel-house, not that I'll mewl, not worth it. All the stories I've told myself, clinging to the putrid mucus, and swelling, swelling, saying, Got it at last, my legend. But why this sudden heat, has anything happened, anything changed? No, the answer is no, I shall never get born and therefore never get dead, and a good job too. And if I tell of me and of that other who is my little one, it is as always for want of love, well I'll be buggered, I wasn't expecting that, want of a homuncule, I can't stop. And yet it sometimes seems to me I did get born and had a long life and met Jackson and wandered in the towns, the woods and wildernesses and tarried by the seas in tears before the islands and peninsulas where night lit the little brief yellow lights of man and all night the great white and colored beams shining in the caves where I was happy, crouched on the sand in the lee of the rocks with the smell of the seaweed and the wet rock and the howling of the wind the waves whipping me with foam or sighing on the beach softly clawing the shingle, no, not happy, I was never that, but wishing night would never end and morning never come when men wake and say, Come on, we'll soon be dead, let's make the most of it. But what matter whether I was born or not, have lived or not, am dead or merely dying, I shall go on doing as I have always done, not knowing what it is I do, nor who I am, nor where I am, nor if I am. Yes, a little creature, I shall try and make a little creature, to hold in my arms, a little creature in my image, no matter what I say. And seeing what a poor thing I have made, or how like myself, I shall eat it. Then be alone a long time, unhappy, not knowing what my prayer should be nor to whom.

I have taken a long time to find him again, but I have found him. How did I know it was he, I don't know. And what can have changed him so? Life perhaps, the struggle to love, to eat, to escape the redressers of wrongs. I slip into him, I suppose in the hope of learning something. But it is a stratum, strata, without debris or vestiges. But before I am done I shall find traces of what was. I ran him down in the heart of the town, sitting on a bench. How did I know it was he? The eyes perhaps. No, I don't know how I knew, I'll take back nothing. Perhaps it is not he. No matter, he is mine now, living flesh and needless to say male, living with that evening life which is like a convalescence, if my memories are mine, and which you savour doddering about in the wake of the fitful sun, or deeper than the dead, in the corridors of the underground railway and the stench of their harassed mobs scurrying from cradle to grave to get to the right place at the right time. What more do I want? Yes, those were the days, quick to night and well beguiled with the search for warmth and reasonably edible scraps. And you imagine it will be so till the end. But suddenly all begins to rage and roar again, you are lost in forests of high threshing ferns or whirled far out on the face of wind-swept wastes, till you begin to wonder if you have not died without knowing and gone to hell or been born again into an even worse place than before. Then it is hard to believe in those brief years when the bakers were often indulgent, at close of day, and baking-apples, I was always a great man for apples, to be had almost for the whinging if you knew your way about, and a little sunshine and shelter for those who direly needed them. And there he is as good as gold on the bench, his back to the river, and dressed as follows, though clothes don't matter, I know, I know, but he'll never have any others, if I know anything about it. He has had them a long time already, to judge by their decay, but no matter, they are the last. But most remarkable of all is his greatcoat, in the sense that it covers him completely and screens him from view. For it is so well buttoned, from top to bottom, by means of fifteen buttons at the very least, set at intervals of three or four inches at the very most, that nothing is to be seen of what goes on inside. And even the two feet, flat on the ground demurely side by side, even they are partly hidden by this coat, in spite of the double flexion of the body, first at the base of the trunk, where the thighs form a right angle with the pelvis, and then again at the knees, where the shins resume the perpendicular. For the posture is completely lacking in abandon, and but for the absence of bonds you might think he was bound to the bench, the posture is so stiff and set in the sharpness of its planes and angles, like that of the Colossus of Memnon, dearly loved son of Dawn. In other words, when he walks, or simply stands stockstill, the tails of this coat literally sweep the ground and rustle like a train, when he walks. And indeed this coat terminates in a fringe, like certain curtains, and the thread of the sleeves too is bare and frayed into long waving strands that flutter in the wind. And the hands too are hidden. For the sleeves of this vast rag are of a piece with its other parts. But the collar has remained intact, being of velvet or perhaps shag. Now as to the color of this coat, for color too is an important consideration, there is no good denying it, all that can be said is that green predominates. And it might safely be wagered that this coat, when new, was of a fine plain green color, what you might call cab green, for there used to be cabs and carriages rattling through the town with panels of a handsome bottle green, I must have seen them myself, and even driven in them, I would not put it past me. But perhaps I am wrong to call this coat a greatcoat and perhaps I should rather call it an overcoat or even cover-me-down, for that is indeed the impression it gives, that it covers the whole body all over, with the exception obviously of the head which emerges, lofty and impassive, clear of its embrace. Yes, passion has marked the face, action too possibly, but it seems to have ceased from suffering, for the time being. But one never knows, does one? Now with regard to the buttons of this coat, they are not so much genuine buttons as little wooden cylinders two or three inches long, with a hole in the middle for the thread, for one hole is ample, though two and even four are more usual, and this because of the inordinate distension of the button-holes consequent on wear and tear. And cylinders is perhaps an exaggeration, for if some of these little sticks or pegs are in fact cylindrical, still more have no definable form. But all are roughly two and a half inches long and thus prevent the lappets from flying apart, all have this feature in common. Now with regard to the material of this coat, all that can be said is that it looks like felt. And the various dints and bulges inflicted upon it by the spasms and contortions of the body subsist long after the fit is past. So much for this coat. I'll tell myself stories about the boots another time, if I can. The hat, as hard as iron, superbly domed above its narrow guttered rim, is marred by a wide crack or rent extending in front from the crown down and intended probably to facilitate the introduction of the skull. For coat and hat have this much in common, that whereas the coat is too big, the hat is too small. And though the edges of the split brim close on the brow like the jaws of a trap, nevertheless the hat is attached, by a string, for safety, to the topmost button of the coat, because, never mind. And were there nothing more to be said about the structure of this hat, the important thing would still remain unsaid, meaning of course its color, of which all that can be said is this, that a strong sun full upon it brings out shimmers of buff and pearl grey and that otherwise it verges on black, without however ever really approaching it. And it would not surprise me to learn that this hat once belonged to a sporting gentleman, a turf-man or breeder of rams. And if we now turn to consider this coat and this hat, no longer separately, but in relation to each other, we are very soon agreeably surprised to see how well they are assorted. And it would not surprise me to learn that they had been bought, one at the hatter's, the other at the tailor's, perhaps the same day and by the same toff, for such men exist, I mean fine handsome men six foot tall and over and all in keeping but the head, small from over-breeding. And it is a pleasure to find oneself again in the presence of one of those immutable relations between harmoniously perishing terms and the effect of which is this, that when weary to death one is almost resigned to—I was going to say to the immortality of the soul, but I don't see the connexion. But to pass on now to the garments that really matter, subjacent and even intimate, all that can be said is that this for the moment is delicate ground. For Sapo—no, I can't call him that any more, and I even wonder how I was able to stomach such a name till now. So then for, let me see, for Macmann, that's not much better but there is no time to lose, for Macmann might be stark staring naked under this surtout for all anyone would be any the wiser. The trouble is he does not stir. Since morning he has been here and now it is

55

evening. The tugs, their black funnels striped with red, tow to their moorings the last barges, freighted with empty barrels. The water cradles already the distant fires of the sunset, orange, rose and green, quenches them in its ruffles and then in trembling pools spreads them bright again. His back is turned to the river, but perhaps it appears to him in the dreadful cries of the gulls that evening assembles, in paroxysms of hunger, round the outflow of the sewers, opposite the Bellevue Hotel. Yes, they too, in a last frenzy before night and its high crags, swoop ravening about the offal. But his face is towards the people that throng the streets at this hour, their long day ended and the whole long evening before them. The doors open and spew them out, each door its contingent. For an instant they cluster in a daze, huddled on the sidewalk or in the gutter, then set off singly on their appointed ways. And even those who know themselves condemned, at the outset, to the same direction, for the choice of directions at the outset is not great, take leave of one another and part, but politely, with some polite excuse, or without a word, for they all know one another's little ways. And God help him who longs, for once, in his recovered freedom, to walk a little way with a fellow-creature, no matter which, unless of course by a merciful chance he stumble on one in the same plight. Then they take a few paces happily side by side, then part, each one muttering perhaps, Now there will be no holding him. At this hour then erotic craving accounts for the majority of couples. But these are few compared to the solitaries pressing forward through the throng, obstructing the access to places of amusement, bowed over the parapets, propped against vacant walls. But soon they come to the appointed place, at home or at some other home, or abroad, as the saying is, in a public place, or in a doorway in view of possible rain. And the first to arrive have seldom long to wait, for all hasten towards one another, knowing how short the time in which to say all the things that lie heavy on the heart and conscience and to do all the things they have to do together, things one cannot do alone. So there they are for a few hours in safety. Then the

56

drowsiness, the little memorandum book with its little special pencil, the yawned goodbyes. Some even take a cab to get more quickly to the rendezvous or, when the fun is over, home or to the hotel, where their comfortable bed is waiting for them. Then you see the last stage of the horse, between its recent career as a pet horse, or a race-horse, or a pack-horse, or a plough-horse, and the shambles. It spends most of its time standing still in an attitude of dejection, its head hanging as low as the shafts and harness permit, that is to say almost to the cobble-stones. But once in motion it is transformed, momentarily, perhaps because of the memories that motion revives, for the mere fact of running and pulling cannot give it much satisfaction, under such conditions. But when the shafts tilt up, announcing that a fare has been taken on board, or when on the contrary the back-hand begins to gall its spine, according as the passenger is seated facing the way he is going or, what is perhaps even more restful, with his back to it, then it rears its head, stiffens its houghs and looks almost content. And you see the cabman too, all alone on his box ten feet from the ground, his knees covered at all seasons and in all weathers with a kind of rug as a rule originally brown, the same precisely which he has just snatched from the rump of his horse. Furious and livid perhaps from want of passengers, the least fare seems to excite him to a frenzy. Then with his huge exasperated hands he tears at the reins or, half rising and leaning out over his horse, brings them down with a crack all along its back. And he launches his equipage blindly through the dark thronging streets, his mouth full of curses. But the passenger, having named the place he wants to go and knowing himself as helpless to act on the course of events as the dark box that encloses him, abandons himself to the pleasant feeling of being freed from all responsibility, or he ponders on what lies before him, or on what lies behind him, saying, Twill not be ever thus, and then in the same breath, But twas ever thus, for there are not five hundred different kinds of passengers. And so they hasten, the horse, the driver and the passenger, towards the appointed place, by

57

the shortest route or deviously, through the press of other misplaced persons. And each one has his reasons, while wondering from time to time what they are worth, and if they are the true ones, for going where he is going rather than somewhere else, and the horse hardly less darkly than the men, though as a rule it will not know where it is going until it gets there, and not always even then. And if as suggested it is dusk, then another phenomenon to be observed is the number of windows and shop-windows that light up an instant, almost after the fashion of the setting sun, though that all depends on the season. But for Macmann, thank God, he's still there, for Macmann it is a true spring evening, an equinoctial gale howls along the quays bordered by high red houses, many of which are warehouses. Or it is perhaps an evening in autumn and these leaves whirling in the air, whence it is impossible to say, for here there are no trees, are perhaps no longer the first of the year, barely green, but old leaves that have known the long joys of summer and now are good for nothing but to lie rottting in a heap, now that men and beasts have no more need of shade, on the contrary, nor birds of nests to lay and hatch out in, and trees must blacken even where no heart beats, though it appears that some stay green forever, for some obscure reason. And it is no doubt all the same to Macmann whether it is spring or whether it is autumn, unless he prefers summer to winter or inversely, which is improbable. But it must not be thought he will never move again, out of this place and attitude, for he has still the whole of his old age before him, and then that kind of epilogue when it is not very clear what is happening and which does not seem to add very much to what has already been acquired or to shed any great light on its confusion, but which no doubt has its usefulness, as hay is left out to dry before being garnered. He will therefore rise, whether he likes it or not, and proceed by other places to another place, and then by others still to yet another, unless he comes back here where he seems to be snug enough, but one never knows, does one? And so on, on, for long years. Because in order not to die you must come and go, come and

58

go, unless you happen to have someone who brings you food wherever you happen to be, like myself. And you can remain for two, three and even four days without stirring hand or foot, but what are four days when you have all old age before you, and then the lingers of evaporation, a drop in the ocean. It is true you know nothing of this, you flatter yourself you are hanging by a thread like all mankind, but that is not the point. For there is no point, no point in not knowing this or that, either you know all or you know nothing, and Macmann knows nothing. But he is concerned only with his ignorance of certain things, of those that appall him among others, which is only human. But it is bad policy, for on the fifth day rise you must, and rise in fact you do, but with how much greater pains than if you had made up your mind to it the day before, or better still two days before, and why add to your pains, it's bad policy, assuming you do add to them, and nothing is less certain. For on the fifth day, when the problem is how to rise, the fourth and third do not matter any more, all that matters is how to rise, for you are half out of your mind. And sometimes you cannot, get to your feet I mean, and have to drag yourself to the nearest plot of vegetables, using the tufts of grass and asperities of the earth to drag yourself forward, or to the nearest clump of brambles, where there are sometimes good things to eat, if acid, and which are superior to the plots in this, that you can crawl into them and hide, as you cannot in a plot of ripe potatoes for example, and in this also, that often you frighten the little wild things away, both furred and feathered. For it is not as if he possessed the means of accumulating, in a single day, enough food to keep him alive for three weeks or a month, and what is a month compared to the whole of second childishness, a drop in a bucket. But he does not, possess them I mean, and could not employ them even if he did, he feels so far from the morrow. And perhaps there is none, no morrow any more, for one who has waited so long for it in vain. And perhaps he has come to that stage of his instant when to live is to wander the last of the living in the depths of an instant without bounds, where the light never changes and the wrecks look all alike. Bluer scarcely than white of egg the eyes stare into the space before them, namely the fulness of the great deep and its unchanging calm. But at long intervals they close, with the gentle suddenness of flesh that tightens, often without anger, and closes on itself. Then you see the old lids all red and worn that seem hard set to meet, for there are four, two for each lachrymal. And perhaps it is then he sees the heaven of the old dream, the heaven of the sea and of the earth too, and the spasms of the waves from shore to shore all stirring to their tiniest stir, and the so different motion of men for example, who are not tied together, but free to come and go as they please. And they make full use of it and come and go, their great balls and sockets rattling and clacking like knackers, each on his way. And when one dies the others go on, as if nothing had happened.

I feel

I feel it's coming. How goes it, thanks, it's coming. I wanted to be quite sure before I noted it. Scrupulous to the last, finical to a fault, that's Malone, all over. I mean sure of feeling that my hour is at hand. For I never doubted it would come, sooner or later, except the days I felt it was past. For my stories are all in vain, deep down I never doubted, even the days abounding in proof to the contrary, that I was still alive and breathing in and out the air of earth. At hand, that is in two or three days, in the language of the days when they taught me the names of the days and I marvelled at their being so few and flourished my little fists, crying out for more, and how to tell the time, and what are two or three days, more or less, in the long run, a joke. But not a word and on with the losing game, it's good for the health. And all I have to do is go on as though doomed to see the midsummer moon. For I believe I have now reached what is called the month of May, I don't know why, I mean why I believe that, for May comes from Maia, hell, I remember that too, goddess of increase and plenty, yes, I believe I have en-

60

tered on the season of increase and plenty, of increase at last, for plenty comes later, with the harvest. So quiet, quiet, I'll be still here at All Saints, in the middle of the chrysanthemums, no, this year I shall not hear them howling over their charnels. But this sensation of dilation is hard to resist. All strains towards the nearest deeps, and notably my feet, which even in the ordinary way are so much further from me than all the rest, from my head I mean, for that is where I am fled, my feet are leagues away. And to call them in, to be cleaned for example, would I think take me over a month, exclusive of the time required to locate them. Strange, I don't feel my feet any more, my feet feel nothing any more, and a mercy it is. And yet I feel they are beyond the range of the most powerful telescope. Is that what is known as having a foot in the grave? And similarly for the rest. For a mere local phenomenon is something I would not have noticed, having been nothing but a series or rather a succession of local phenomena all my life, without any result. But my fingers too write in other latitudes and the air that breathes through my pages and turns them without my knowing, when I doze off, so that the subject falls far from the verb and the object lands somewhere in the void, is not the air of this second-last abode, and a mercy it is. And perhaps on my hands it is the shimmer of the shadows of leaves and flowers and the brightness of a forgotten sun. Now my sex, I mean the tube itself, and in particular the nozzle, from which when I was yet a virgin clouts and gouts of sperm came streaming and splashing up into my face, a continuous flow, while it lasted, and which must still drip a little piss from time to time, otherwise I would be dead of uraemia, I do not expect to see my sex again, with my naked eye, not that I wish to, we've stared at each other long enough, in the eye, but it gives you some idea. But that is not all and my extremities are not the only parts to recede, in their respective directions, far from it. For my arse for example, which can hardly be accused of being the end of anything, if my arse suddenly started to shit at the present moment, which God forbid, I firmly believe the lumps would fall out in

Australia. And if I were to stand up again, from which God preserve me, I fancy I would fill a considerable part of the universe, oh not more than lying down, but more noticeably. For it is a thing I have often noticed, the best way to pass unnoticed is to lie down flat and not move. And so there I am, who always thought I would shrivel and shrivel, more and more, until in the end I could be almost buried in a casket, swelling. No matter, what matters is that in spite of my stories I continue to fit in this room, let us call it a room, that's all that matters, and I need not worry, I'll fit in it as long as needs be. And if I ever succeed in breathing my last it will not be in the street, or in a hospital, but here, in the midst of my possessions, beside this window that sometimes looks as if it were painted on the wall, like Tiepolo's ceiling at Würzburg, what a tourist I must have been, I even remember the diaeresis, if it is one. If only I could be sure, of my deathbed I mean. And yet how often I have seen this old head swing out through the door, low, for my big old bones weigh heavy, and the door is low, lower and lower in my opinion. And each time it bangs against the jamb, my head does, for I am tall, and the landing is small, and the man carrying my feet cannot wait, before he starts down the stairs, for the whole of me to be out, on the landing I mean, but he has to start turning before that, so as not to bang into the wall, of the landing I mean. So my head bangs against the jamb, it's inevitable. And it doesn't matter to my head, in the state it is in, but the man carrying it says, Eh Bob easy!, out of respect perhaps, for he doesn't know me, he didn't know me, or for fear of hurting his fingers. Bang! Easy! Right! The door!, and the room is vacant at last and ready to receive, after disinfection, for you can't be too careful, a large family or a pair of turtle doves. Yes, the event is past, but it's too soon to use it, hence the delay, that's what I tell myself. But I tell myself so many things, what truth is there in all this babble? I don't know. I simply believe I can say nothing that is not true, I mean that has not happened, it's not the same thing but no matter. Yes, that's what I like about me, at least one of the things, that I can say, Up the Republic!, for example, or, Sweetheart!, for example, without having to wonder if I should not rather have cut my tongue out, or said something else. Yes, no reflection is needed, before or after, I have only to open my mouth for it to testify to the old story, my old story, and to the long silence that has silenced me, so that all is silent. And if I ever stop talking it will be because there is nothing more to be said, even though all has not been said, even though nothing has been said. But let us leave these morbid matters and get on with that of my demise, in two or three days if I remember rightly. Then it will be all over with the Murphys, Merciers, Molloys, Morans and Malones, unless it goes on beyond the grave. But sufficient unto the day, let us first defunge, then we'll see. How many have I killed, hitting them on the head or setting fire to them? Off-hand I can only think of four, all unknowns, I never knew anyone. A sudden wish, I have a sudden wish to see, as sometimes in the old days, something, anything, no matter what, something I could not have imagined. There was the old butler too, in London I think, there's London again, I cut his throat with his razor, that makes five. It seems to me he had a name. Yes, what I need now is a touch of the unimaginable, coloured for preference, that would do me good. For this may well be my last journey, down the long familiar galleries, with my little suns and moons that I hang aloft and my pockets full of pebbles to stand for men and their seasons, my last, if I'm lucky. Then back here, to me, whatever that means, and no more leaving me, no more asking me for what I haven't got. Or perhaps we'll all come back, reunited, done with parting, done with prying on one another, back to this foul little den all dirty white and vaulted, as though hollowed out of ivory, an old rotten tooth. Or alone, back alone, as alone as when I went, but I doubt it, I can hear them from here, clamouring after me down the corridors, stumbling through the rubble, beseeching me to take them with me. That settles that. I have just time, if I have calculated right, and if I have calculated wrong so much the better, I ask nothing better, besides I haven't calculated anything, don't ask anything either, just time to go and take a little turn, come back here and do all I have to do, I forgot what, ah yes, put my possessions in order, and then something else, I forget what, but it will come back to me when the time comes. But before I go I should like to find a hole in the wall behind which so much goes on, such extraordinary things, and often coloured. One last glimpse and I feel I could slip away as happy as if I were embarking for—I nearly said for Cythera, decidedly it is time for this to stop. After all this window is whatever I want it to be, up to a point, that's right, don't compromise yourself. What strikes me to begin with is how much rounder it is than it was, so that it looks like a bull's-eye, or a porthole. No matter, provided there is something on the other side. First I see the night, which surprises me, to my surprise, I suppose because I want to be surprised, just once more. For in the room it is not night, I know, here it is never really night, I don't care what I said, but often darker than now, whereas out there up in the sky it is black night, with few stars, just enough to show that the black night I see is truly of mankind and not merely painted on the window-pane, for they tremble, like true stars, as they would not do if they were painted. And as if that were not enough to satisfy me it is the outer world, the other world, suddenly the window across the way lights up, or suddenly I realize it is lit up, for I am not one of those people who can take in everything at a single glance, but I have to look long and fixedly and give things time to travel the long road that lies between me and them. And that indeed is a happy chance and augurs well, unless it be devised on purpose to make mock of me, for I might have found nothing better to speed me from this place than the nocturnal sky where nothing happens, though it is full of tumult and violence, nothing unless you have the whole night before you to follow the slow fall and rise of other worlds, when there are any, or watch out for the meteors, and I have not the whole night before me. And it does not matter to me whether they have risen before dawn, or not yet gone to bed, or risen in the middle of the night intending perhaps to go back to bed when they have finished, and it is enough for me to see them standing up against each other behind the curtain, which is dark, so that it is a dark light, if one may say so, and dim the shadow they cast. For they cleave so fast together that they seem a single body, and consequently a single shadow. But when they totter it is clear they are twain, and in vain they clasp with the energy of despair, it is clear we have here two distinct and separate bodies, each enclosed within its own frontiers, and having no need of each other to come and go and sustain the flame of life, for each is well able to do so, independently of the other. Perhaps they are cold, that they rub against each other so, for friction maintains heat and brings it back when it is gone. It is all very pretty and strange, this big complicated shape made up of more than one, for perhaps there are three of them, and how it sways and totters, but rather poor in colour. But the night must be warm, for of a sudden the curtain lifts on a flare of tender colour, pale blush and white of flesh, then pink that must come from a garment and gold too that I haven't time to understand. So it is not cold they are, standing so lightly clad by the open window. Ah how stupid I am, I see what it is, they must be loving each other, that must be how it is done. Good, that has done me good. I'll see now if the sky is still there, then go. They are right up against the curtain now, motionless. Is it possible they have finished already? They have loved each other standing, like dogs. Soon they will be able to part. Or perhaps they are just having a breather, before they tackle the titbit. Back and forth, back and forth, that must be wonderful. They seem to be in pain. Enough, enough, goodbye.

Caught by the rain far from shelter Macmann stopped and lay down, saying, The surface thus pressed against the ground will remain dry, whereas standing I would get uniformly wet all over, as if rain were a mere matter of drops per hour, like electricity. So he lay down, prostrate, after a moment's hesitation, for he could just as easily have lain down supine or, meeting himself half-way, on one of his two sides. But he fancied that the nape of the neck and the back right down to the loins were more vulnerable than the chest and belly, not realizing, any more than if he had been a crate of tomatoes, that all these parts are intimately and even indissolubly bound up together, at least until death do them part, and to many another too of which he had no conception, and that a drop of water out of season on the coccyx for example may lead to spasms of the risorius lasting for years as when, having waded through a bog, you merely die of pneumonia and your legs none the worse for the wetting, but if anything better, thanks perhaps to the action of the bog-water. It was a heavy, cold and perpendicular rain, which led Macmann to suppose it would be brief, as if there were a relation between violence and duration, and that he would spring to his feet in ten minutes or a quarter of an hour, his front, no, his back, white with, no, front was right, his front white with dust. This is the kind of story he has been telling himself all his life, saying, This cannot possibly last much longer. It was sometime in the afternoon, impossible to say more, for hours and hours past it had been the same leaden light, so it was very probably the afternoon, very. The still air, though not cold as in winter, seemed without promise or memory of warmth. Incommoded by the rain pouring into his hat through the crack, Macmann took it off and laid it on his temple, that is to say turned his head and pressed his cheek to the ground. His hands at the ends of the long outstretched arms clutched the grass, each hand a tuft, with as much energy as if he had been spread-eagled against the face of a cliff. Let us by all means continue this description. The rain pelted down on his back with the sound first of a drum, but in a short time of washing, as when washing is soused gurgling and squelching in a tub, and he distinguished clearly and with interest the difference in noise of the rain falling on him and falling on the earth. For his ear, which is on the same plane as the cheek or nearly, was glued to the earth in a way it seldom is in wet weather, and he could hear the kind of distant roar of the earth drinking and the sighing of the soaked bowed grasses. The idea of punishment came to his mind, addicted it is true to that chimera and probably impressed by the posture of the body and the fingers clenched as though in torment. And without knowing exactly what his sin was he felt full well that living was not a sufficient atonement for it or that this atonement was in itself a sin, calling for more atonement, and so on, as if there could be anything but life, for the living. And no doubt he would have wondered if it was really necessary to be guilty in order to be punished but for the memory, more and more galling, of his having consented to live in his mother, then to leave her. And this again he could not see as his true sin, but as yet another atonement which had miscarried and, far from cleansing him of his sin, plunged him in it deeper than before. And truth to tell the ideas of guilt and punishment were confused together in his mind, as those of cause and effect so often are in the minds of those who continue to think. And it was often in fear and trembling that he suffered, saying, This will cost me dear. But not knowing how to go about it, in order to think and feel correctly, he would suddenly begin to smile for no reason, as now, as then, for already it is long since that afternoon, in March perhaps, or in November perhaps, in October rather, when the rain caught him far from shelter, to smile and give thanks for the teeming rain and the promise it contained of stars a little later, to light his way and enable him to get his bearings, should he wish to do so. For he did not know quite where he was, except that he was in a plain, and the mountains not far, nor the sea, nor the town, and that all he needed was a dust of light and a few fixed stars to enable him to make definite headway towards the one, or the other, or the third, or to hold fast where he was, in the plain, as he might be pleased to decide. For in order to hold fast in the place where you happen to be you need light too, unless you go round in circles, which is practically impossible in the dark, or halt and wait, motionless, for day to dawn again, and then you die of cold, unless it does not happen to be cold. But Macmann would have been more than human, after forty or forty-five minutes of sanguine expectation, seeing the rain persist as heavy as ever and day recede at last, if he had not begun to reproach himself with what he had done, namely with having lain down on the ground instead of continuing on his course, in as straight a line as possible, in the hope of chancing sooner or later on a tree, or a ruin. And instead of being astonished at such long and violent rain, he was astonished at not having understood, from the moment the first timid drops began to fall, that it was going to rain violently and long and that he must not stop and lie down, but on the contrary press forward, as fast as his legs could carry him, for he was no more than human, than the son and grandson and greatgrandson of humans. But between him and those grave and sober men, first bearded, then moustached, there was this difference, that his semen had never done any harm to anyone. So his link with his species was through his ascendants only, who were all dead, in the fond hope they had perpetuated themselves. But the better late than never thanks to which true men, true links, can acknowledge the error of their ways and hasten on to the next, was beyond the power of Macmann, to whom it sometimes seemed that he could grovel and wallow in his mortality until the end of time and not have done. And without going so far as that, he who has waited long enough will wait for ever. And there comes the hour when nothing more can happen and nobody more can come and all is ended but the waiting that knows itself in vain. Perhaps he had come to that. And when (for example) you die, it is too late, you have been waiting too long, you are no longer sufficiently alive to be able to stop. Perhaps he had come to that. But apparently not, though acts don't matter, I know, I know, nor thoughts. For having reproached himself with what he had done, and with his monstrous error of appreciation, instead of springing up and hurrying on he turned over on his back, thus offering all his front to the deluge. And it was then his hair appeared clearly for the first time since his walks bareheaded in the smiling haunts of his youth, his hat having remained in the place which his head had just left. For when, lying on your stomach in a wild and practically illimitable part of the country, you turn over on your back, then there is a sideways movement of the whole body. including the head, unless you make a point of avoiding it, and the head comes to rest at x inches approximately from where it was before, x being the width of the shoulders in inches, for the head is right in the middle of the shoulders. But when you are in a narrow bed, I mean one just wide enough to contain you, a pallet shall we say, then it is in vain you turn over on your back, then back over on your stomach, the head remains always in the same place, unless you make a point of inclining it to the right or to the left, and some there doubtless are who go to this trouble, in the hope of finding a little freshness. He tried to look at the dark streaming mass which was all that remained of sky and air, but the rain hurt his eyes and shut them. He opened his mouth and lay for a long time thus, his mouth open and his hands also and as far apart as possible from each other. For it is a curious thing, one tends less to clutch the ground when on one's back than when on one's stomach, there is a curious remark which might be worth following up. And just as an hour before he had pulled up his sleeves the better to clutch the grass, so now he pulled them up again the better to feel the rain pelting down on his palms, also called the hollows of the hands, or the flats, it all depends. And in the midst—but I was nearly forgetting the hair, which from the point of view of colour was to white very much as the hour's gloom to black and from the point of view of length very long what is more, very long behind and very long on either side. And on a dry and windy day it would have gone romping in the grass almost like grass itself. But the rain glued it to the ground and churned it up with the earth and grass into a kind of muddy pulp, not a muddy pulp, a kind of muddy pulp. And in the midst of his suffering, for one does not remain so long in such a position without being incommoded, he began to wish that the rain would never cease nor consequently his sufferings or pain, for the cause of his pain was almost certainly the rain, recumbency in itself not being particularly unpleasant, as if there existed a relation between that which suffers and that which causes to suffer. For the rain could cease without his ceasing to suffer, just as he could cease to suffer without the rain's ceasing on that account. And on him already this important quarter-truth was perhaps beginning to dawn. For while deploring he could not spend the rest of his life (which would thereby have been agreeably abridged) under this heavy, cold (without being icy) and perpendicular rain, now supine, now prone, he was quarter-inclined to wonder if he was not mistaken in holding it responsible for his sufferings and if in reality his discomfort was not the effect of quite a different cause or set of causes. For people are never content to suffer, but they must have heat and cold, rain and its contrary which is fine weather, and with that love, friendship, black skin and sexual and peptic deficiency for example, in short the furies and frenzies happily too numerous to be numbered of the body including the skull and its annexes, whatever that means, such as the club-foot, in order that they may know very precisely what exactly it is that dares prevent their happiness from being unalloyed. And sticklers have been met with who had no peace until they knew for certain whether their carcinoma was of the pylorus or whether on the contrary it was not rather of the duodenum. But these are flights for which Macmann was not yet fledged, and indeed he was rather of the earth earthy and ill-fitted for pure reason, especially in the circumstances in which we have been fortunate enough to circumscribe him. And to tell the truth he was by temperament more reptile than bird and could suffer extensive mutilation and survive, happier sitting than standing and lying down than sitting, so that he sat and lay down at the least pretext and only rose again when the élan vital or struggle for life began to prod him in the arse again. And a good half of his existence must have been spent in a motionlessness akin to that of stone, not to say the three quarters, or even the four fifths, a motionlessness at first skin-deep, but which little by little invaded, I will not say the vital parts, but at least the sensibility and understanding. And it must be presumed that he received from his numerous forbears, through the agency of his papa and his mama, a cast-iron vegetative system, to have reached the age he has just reached and which is nothing or very little compared to the age he will reach, as I know to my cost, without any serious mishap, I mean one of a nature to carry him off on the spot. For no one ever came to his help, to help him avoid the thorns and snares that attend the steps of innocence, and he could never count on any other craft than his own, any other strength, to go from morning to evening and then from evening to morning without mortal hurt. And notably he never received any gifts of cash, or very seldom, and very paltry, which would not have mattered if he had been able to earn, in the sweat of his brow or by making use of his intelligence. But when given the job of weeding a plot of young carrots for example, at the rate of threepence or even sixpence an hour, it often happened that he tore them all up, through absent-mindedness, or carried away by I know not what irresistible urge that came over him at the sight of vegetables, and even of flowers, and literally blinded him to his true interests, the urge to make a clean sweep and have nothing before his eyes but a patch of brown earth rid of its parasites, it was often more than he could resist. Or without going so far as that, suddenly all swam before his eyes, he could no longer distinguish the plants destined for the embellishment of the home or the nutrition of man and beast from the weeds which are said to serve no useful purpose, but which must have their usefulness too, for the earth to favour them so, such as squitch beloved of dogs and from which man too in his turn has succeeded in extracting a brew, and the hoe fell from his hands. And even with such humble occupations as street-cleaning to which with hopefulness he had sometimes turned, on the off chance of his being a born scavenger, he did not succeed any better. And even he himself was compelled to admit that the place swept by him looked dirtier at his departure than on his arrival, as if a demon had driven him to collect, with the broom, shovel and barrow placed gratis at his disposal by the corporation, all the dirt and filth which chance had withdrawn from the sight of the tax-payer and add them thus recovered to those already visible and which he was

71

employed to remove. With the result that at the end of the day, throughout the sector consigned to him, one could see the peels of oranges and bananas, cigarette-butts, unspeakable scraps of paper, dogs' and horses' excrement and other muck, carefully concentrated all along the sidewalk or distributed on the crown of the street, as though in order to inspire the greatest possible disgust in the passers-by or provoke the greatest possible number of accidents, some fatal, by means of the slip. And yet he had done his honest best to give satisfaction, taking as his model his more experienced colleagues, and doing as they did. But it was truly as if he were not master of his movements and did not know what he was doing, while he was doing it, nor what he had done, once he had done it. For someone had to say to him, Look at what you have done, sticking his nose in it so to speak, otherwise he did not realize, but thought he had done as any man of good will would have done in his place and with very much the same results, in spite of his lack of experience. And yet when it came to doing some little thing for himself, as for example when he had to repair or replace one of his buttons or pegs, which were not long-lived being mostly of green wood and exposed to all the rigours of the temperate zone, then he really exhibited a certain dexterity, without the help of any other apparatus than his bare hands. And indeed he had devoted to these little tasks a great part of his existence, that it is to say of the half or quarter of his existence associated with more or less coordinated movements of the body. For he had to, he had to, if he wished to go on coming and going on the earth, which to tell the truth he did not, particularly, but he had to, for obscure reasons known who knows to God alone, though to tell the truth God does not seem to need reasons for doing what he does, and for omitting to do what he omits to do, to the same degree as his creatures, does he? Such then seemed to be Macmann, seen from a certain angle, incapable of weeding a bed of pansies or marigolds and leaving one standing and at the same time well able to consolidate his boots with willow bark and thongs of wicker, so that he might come and go on the earth from time to time and

72

not wound himself too sorely on the stones, thorns and broken glass provided by the carelessness or wickedness of man, with hardly a complaint, for he had to. For he was incapable of picking his steps and choosing where to put down his feet (which would have permitted him to go barefoot). And even had he been so he would have been so to no great purpose, so little was he master of his movements. And what is the good of aiming at the smooth and mossy places when the foot, missing its mark, comes down on the flints and shards or sinks up to the knee in the cowpads? But to pass on now to considerations of another order, it is perhaps not inappropriate to wish Macmann, since wishing costs nothing, sooner or later a general paralysis sparing at a pinch the arms if that is conceivable, in a place impermeable as far as possible to wind, rain, sound, cold, great heat (as in the seventh century) and daylight, with one or two eiderdowns just in case and a charitable soul say once a week bearing eating-apples and sardines in oil for the purpose of postponing as long as possible the fatal hour, it would be wonderful. But in the meantime in the end, the rain still falling with unabated violence in spite of his having turned over on his back, Macmann grew restless, flinging himself from side to side as though in a fit of the fever, buttoning himself and unbuttoning and finally rolling over and over in the same direction, it little matters which, with a brief pause after each roll to begin with, and then without break. And in theory his hat should have followed him, seeing it was tied to his coat, and the string twisted itself about his neck, but not at all, for theory is one thing and reality another, and the hat remained where it was, I mean in its place, like a thing forsaken. But perhaps one day a high wind would come and send it, dry and light again, bowling and bounding over the plain until it came to the town, or the ocean, but not necessarily. Now it was not the first time that Macmann rolled upon the ground, but he had always done so without ulterior locomotive motive. Whereas then, as he moved further and further from the place where the rain had caught him far from shelter and which thanks to the hat continued to contrast with the surrounding space, he realized he was advancing with regularity, and even a certain rapidity, along the arc of a gigantic circle probably, for he assumed that one of his extremities was heavier than the other, without knowing quite which, but not by much. And as he rolled he conceived and polished the plan of continuing to roll on all night if necessary, or at least until his strength should fail him, and thus approach the confines of this plain which to tell the truth he was in no hurry to leave, but nevertheless was leaving, he knew it. And without reducing his speed he began to dream of a flat land where he would never have to rise again and hold himself erect in equilibrium, first on the right foot for example, then on the left, and where he might come and go and so survive after the fashion of a great cylinder endowed with the faculties of cognition and volition. And without exactly building castles in Spain, for that

Quick quick my possessions. Quiet, quiet, twice, I have time, lots of time, as usual. My pencil, my two pencils, the one of which nothing remains between my huge fingers but the lead fallen from the wood and the other, long and round, in the bed somewhere, I was holding it in reserve, I won't look for it, I know it's there somewhere, if I have time when I've finished I'll look for it, if I don't find it I won't have it, I'll make the correction, with the other, if anything remains of it. Quiet, quiet. My exercise-book, I don't see it, but I feel it in my left hand, I don't know where it comes from, I didn't have it when I came here, but I feel it is mine. That's the style, as if I were sweet and seventy. In that case the bed would be mine too, and the little table, the dish, the pots, the cupboard, the blankets. No, nothing of all that is mine. But the exercise-book is mine, I can't explain. The two pencils then, the exercise-book and then the stick, which I did not have either when I came here, but which I consider mine, I must have described it long ago. I am quiet, I have time, but I shall describe as little as possible. It is with me in the bed, under the blankets, there was a time I

74

used to rub myself against it, saying, It's a little woman. But it is so long that it sticks out under the pillow and finishes far behind me. I continue from memory. It is black dark. I can hardly see the window. It must be letting in the night again. Even if I had time to rummage in my possessions, to bring them over to the bed one by one or tangled together as is often the way with forsaken things, I would not see anything. And perhaps indeed I have the time, let us assume I have the time, and proceed as if I had not. But it cannot be so long since I checked and went through all my things, in the light, in anticipation of this hour. But since then I must have forgotten it all. A needle stuck into two corks to prevent it from sticking into me, for if the point pricks less than the eye, no, that's wrong, for if the point pricks more than the eye, the eye pricks too, that's wrong too. Round the shank, between the two corks, a wisp of black thread clings. It is a pretty little object, like a— no, it is like nothing. The bowl of my pipe, though I never used a tobacco-pipe. I must have found it somewhere, on the ground, when out walking. There it was, in the grass, thrown away because it could no longer serve, the stem having broken off (I suddenly remember that) just short of the bowl. This pipe could have been repaired, but he must have said, Bah, I'll buy myself another. But all I found was the bowl. But all that is mere supposition. Perhaps I thought it pretty, or felt for it that foul feeling of pity I have so often felt in the presence of things, especially little portable things in wood and stone, and which made me wish to have them about me and keep them always, so that I stooped and picked them up and put them in my pocket, often with tears, for I wept up to a great age, never having really evolved in the fields of affection and passion, in spite of my experiences. And but for the company of these little objects which I picked up here and there, when out walking, and which sometimes gave me the impression that they too needed me, I might have been reduced to the society of nice people or to the consolations of some religion or other, but I think not. And I loved, I remember, as I walked along, with

F

my hands deep in my pockets, for I am trying to speak of the time when I could still walk without a stick and a fortiori without crutches, I loved to finger and caress the hard shapely objects that were there in my deep pockets, it was my way of talking to them and reassuring them. And I loved to fall asleep holding in my hand a stone, a horse chestnut or a cone, and I would be still holding it when I woke. my fingers closed over it, in spite of sleep which makes a rag of the body, so that it may rest. And those of which I wearied, or which were ousted by new loves, I threw away, that is to say I cast round for a place to lay them where they would be at peace forever, and no one ever find them short of an extraordinary hazard, and such places are few and far between, and I laid them there. Or I buried them, or threw them into the sea, with all my strength as far as possible from the land, those I knew for certain would not float, even briefly. But many a wooden friend too I have sent to the bottom, weighted with a stone. Until I realized it was wrong of me. For when the string is rotted they will rise to the surface, if they have not already done so, and return to the land, sooner or later. In this way I disposed of things I loved but could no longer keep, because of new loves. And often I missed them. But I had hidden them so well that even I could never find them again. That's the style, as if I still had time to kill. And so I have, deep down I know it well. Then why play at being in a hurry? I don't know. Perhaps I am in a hurry after all, it was the impression I had a short time ago. But my impressions. And what after all if I were not so anxious as I make out to recall to mind all that is left to me of all I ever had, a good dozen objects at least to put it mildly? No no, I must. Then it's something else. Where were we? My bowl. So I never got rid of it. I used it as a receptacle, I kept things in it, I wonder what I could have kept in it, so small a space, and I made a little cap for it, out of tin. Next. Poor Macmann. Decidedly it will never have been given to me to finish anything, except perhaps breathing. One must not be greedy. But is this how one chokes? Presumably. And the rattle, what about the rattle? Perhaps it is not de rigueur after all. To have vagitated and not be bloody well able to rattle. How life dulls the power to protest to be sure. I wonder what my last words will be, written, the others do not endure, but vanish, into thin air. I shall never know. I shall not finish this inventory either, a little bird tells me so, the paraclete perhaps, psittaceously named. Be it so. A club in any case, I can't help it, I must state the facts, without trying to understand, to the end. There are moments when I feel I have been here always, perhaps even was born here. Then it passes. That would explain many things. Or that I have come back after a long absence. But I have done with feelings and hypotheses. This club is mine and that is all about it. It is stained with blood, but insufficiently, insufficiently. I have defended myself, ill, but I have defended myself. That is what I tell myself sometimes. One boot, originally yellow, I forget for which foot. The other, its fellow, has gone. They took it away, at the beginning, before they realized I should never walk again. And they left the other, in the hope I would be saddened, seeing it there, without its fellow. Men are like that. Or perhaps it is on top of the cupboard. I have looked for it everywhere, with my stick, but I never thought of the top of the cupboard. Till now. And as I shall never look for it any more, or for anything else, either on top of the cupboard or anywhere else, it is no longer mine. For only those things are mine the whereabouts of which I know well enough to be able to lay hold of them, if necessary, that is the definition I have adopted, to define my possessions. For otherwise there would be no end to it. But in any case there will be no end to it. It did not greatly resemble—but it is wrong of me to dwell upon it—the one I have preserved, the yellow one, remarkable for the number of its eyeholes, I never saw a boot with so many eyeholes, useless for the most part, having ceased to be holes, and become slits. All these things are together in the corner in a heap. I could lay hold of them, even now, in the dark, I need only wish to do so. I would identify them by touch, the message would flow all along the stick, I would hook the desired object and bring it over to the bed, I would hear it coming to-wards me over the floor, gliding, jogging, less and less dear, I would hoist it up on the bed in such a way as not to break the window or damage the ceiling, and at last I would have it in my hands. If it was my hat I might put it on, that would remind me of the good old days, though I remember them sufficiently well. It has lost its brim, it looks like a bell-glass to put over a melon. In order to put it on and take it off you have to grasp it like a great ball, between your palms. It is perhaps the only object in my possession the history of which I have not for-gotten, I mean counting from the day it became mine. I know in what circumstances it lost its brim, I was there at the time, it was so that I might keep it on while I slept. I should rather like it to be buried with me, a harmless whim, but what steps should I take? Mem, put it on on the off chance, well wedged down, before it is too late. But all in due time. Should I go on I wonder. I feel I am perhaps attributing to myself things I no longer possess and reporting as missing others that are not missing. And I feel there are others, over there in the corner, belonging to a third category, that of those of which I know nothing and with regard to which therefore there is little danger of my being wrong, or of my being right. And I remind myself also that since I last went through my possessions much water has passed beneath Butt Bridge, in both directions. For I have sufficiently perished in this room to know that some things go out, and other things come in, through I know not what agency. And among those that go out there are some that come back, after a more or less prolonged absence, and others that never come back. With the result that, among those that come in, some are familiar to me, others not. I don't understand. And, stranger still, there exists a whole family of objects, having ap-parently very little in common, which have never left me, since I have been here, but remained quietly in their place, in the corner, as in any ordinary uninhabited room. Or else they were very quick. How false all that rings. But there is no guarantee things will be ever thus. I cannot account in any other way for the changing aspect of my possessions. So that, strictly speaking, it is impossible for me to know, from one moment to the next, what is mine and what is not, according to my definition. So I wonder if I should go on, I mean go on drawing up an inventory corresponding perhaps but faintly to the facts, and if I should not rather cut it short and devote myself to some other form of distraction, of less consequence, or simply wait, doing nothing, or counting perhaps, one, two, three and so on, until all danger to myself from myself is past at last. That is what comes of being scrupulous. If I had a penny I would let it make up my mind. Decidedly the night is long and poor in counsel. Perhaps I should persist until dawn. All things considered. Good idea, excellent. If at dawn I am still there I shall take a decision. I am half asleep. But I dare not sleep. Rectifications in extremis, in extremissimis, are always possible after all. But have I not perhaps just passed away? Malone, Malone, no more of that. Perhaps I should call in all my possessions such as they are and take them into bed with me. Would that be of any use? I suppose not. But I may. I have always that resource. When it is light enough to see. Then I shall have them all round me, on top of me, under me, in the corner there will be nothing left, all will be in the bed, with me. I shall hold my photograph in my hand, my stone, so that they can't get away. I shall put on my hat. Perhaps I shall have something in my mouth, my scrap of newspaper perhaps, or my buttons, and I shall be lying on other treasures still. My photograph. It is not a photograph of me, but I am perhaps at hand. It is an ass, taken from in front and close up, at the edge of the ocean, it is not the ocean, but for me it is the ocean. They naturally tried to make it raise its head, so that its beautiful eyes might be impressed on the celluloid, but it holds it lowered. You can tell by its ears that it is not pleased. They put a boater on its head. The thin hard parallel legs, the little hooves light and dainty on the sand. The outline is blurred, that's the operator's giggle shaking the camera. The ocean looks so unnatural that you'd think you were in a studio, but is it not rather the reverse I should say? No trace left of any clothes for example, apart from the boot, the hat and three socks, I counted them. Where have my clothes disappeared, my greatcoat, my trousers and the flannel that Mr. Quin gave me, with the remark that he did not need it any more? Perhaps they were burnt. But our business is not with what I have no longer, such things do not count at such a moment, whatever people may say. In any case I think I'll stop. I was keeping the best for the end, but I don't feel very well, perhaps I'm going, that would surprise me. It is a passing weakness, everyone has experienced that. One weakens, then it passes, one's strength comes back and one resumes. That is probably what is happening to me. I yawn, would I yawn if it was serious? Why not? I would gladly eat a little soup, if there was any left. No, even if there was some left I would not eat it. So there. It is some days now since my soup was renewed, did I mention that? I suppose so. It is in vain I dispatch my table to the door, bring it back beside me, move it to and fro in the hope that the noise will be heard and correctly interpreted in the right quarters, the dish remains empty. One of the pots on the other hand remains full, and the other is filling slowly. If I ever succeed in filling it I shall empty them both out on the floor, but it is unlikely. Now that I have stopped eating I produce less waste and so eliminate less. The pots do not seem to be mine, I simply have the use of them. They answer to the definition of what is mine, but they are not mine. Perhaps it is the definition that is at fault. They have each two handles or ears, projecting above the rim and facing each other, into which I insert my stick. In this way I move my pots about, lift them up and set them down. Nothing has been left to chance. Or is it a happy chance? I can therefore easily turn them upside down, if I am driven to it, and wait for them to empty, as long as necessary. After this passing reference to my pots I feel a little more lively. They are not mine, but I say my pots, as I say my bed, my window, as I say me. Nevertheless I shall stop. It is my possessions have weakened me, if I start talking about them again I shall weaken again, for the same causes give rise to the same effects. I should have liked to speak of the cap of my bicycle-bell, of my half-crutch, the top half, you'd think it was a baby's crutch. But I can still do so, what is there to prevent me? I don't know. I can't. To think I shall perhaps die of hunger, after all, of starvation rather, after having struggled successfully all my life against that menace. I can't believe it. There is a providence for impotent old men, to the end. And when they cannot swallow any more someone rams a tube down their gullet, or up their rectum, and fills them full of vitaminized pap, so as not to be accused of murder. I shall therefore die of old age pure and simple, glutted with days as in the days before the flood, on a full stomach. Perhaps they think I am dead. Or perhaps they are dead themselves. I say they, though perhaps I should not. In the beginning, but was it the beginning, I used to see an old woman, then for a time an old yellow arm, then for a time an old yellow hand. But these were probably no more than the agents of a consortium. And indeed the silence at times is such that the earth seems uninhabited. That is what comes of the taste for generalisation. You have only to hear nothing for a few days, in your hole, nothing but the sounds of things, and you begin to fancy yourself the last of human kind. What if I started to scream? Not that I wish to draw attention to myself, simply to try and find out if there is someone about. But I don't like screaming. I have spoken softly, gone my ways softly, all my days, as behoves one who has nothing to say, nowhere to go, and so nothing to gain by being seen or heard. Not to mention the possibility of there being not a living soul within a radius of one hundred yards and then such multitudes of people that they are walking on top of one another. They do not dare come near me. In that case I could scream my head off to no purpose. I shall try all the same. I have tried. I heard nothing out of the ordinary. No, I exaggerate, I heard a kind of burning croak deep down in the windpipe, as when one has heartburn. With practice I might produce a groan, before I die. I am not sleepy any more. In any case I must not sleep any more. What tedium. I have missed the ebb. Did I say I only say a small proportion of the

81

things that come into my head? I must have. I choose those that seem somehow akin. It is not always easy. I hope they are the most important. I wonder if I shall ever be able to stop. Perhaps I should throw away my lead. I could never retrieve it now. I might be sorry. My little lead. It is a risk I do not feel inclined to take, just now. What then? I wonder if I could not contrive, wielding my stick like a punt-pole, to move my bed. It may well be on castors, many beds are. Incredible I should never have thought of this, all the time I have been here. I might even succeed in steering it, it is so narrow, through the door, and even down the stairs, if there is a stairs that goes down. To be off and away. The dark is against me, in a sense. But I can always try and see if the bed will move. I have only to set the stick against the wall and push. And I can see myself already, if successful, taking a little turn in the room, until it is light enough for me to set forth. At least while thus employed I shall stop telling myself lies. And then, who knows, the physical effort may polish me off, by means of heart failure.

I have lost my stick, That is the outstanding event of the day, for it is day again. The bed has not stirred. I must have missed my point of purchase, in the dark. Sine qua non, Archimedes was right. The stick, having slipped, would have plucked me from the bed if I had not let it go. It would of course have been better for me to relinquish my bed than to lose my stick. But I had not time to think. The fear of falling is the source of many a folly. It is a disaster. I suppose the wisest thing now is to live it over again, meditate upon it and be edified. It is thus that man distinguishes himself from the ape and rises, from discovery to discovery, ever higher, towards the light. Now that I have lost my stick I realize what it is I have lost and all it meant to me. And thence ascend, painfully, to an understanding of the Stick, shorn of all its accidents, such as I had never dreamt of. What a broadening of the mind. So that I half discern, in the veritable catastrophe that has befallen me, a blessing in disguise. How comforting that is. Catastrophe too in the ancient sense no doubt. To be buried in lava and not turn a hair, it is then a man shows what stuff he is made of. To know you can do better next time, unrecognizably better, and that there is no next time, and that it is a blessing there is not, there is a thought to be going on with. I thought I was turning my stick to the best possible account, like a monkey scratching its fleas with the key that opens its cage. For it is obvious to me now that by making a more intelligent use of my stick I might have extracted myself from my bed and perhaps even got myself back into it, when tired of rolling and dragging myself about the floor or on the stairs. That would have introduced a little variety into my decomposition. How is it that never occurred to me? It is true I had no wish to leave my bed. But can the sage have no wish for something the very possibility of which he does not conceive? I don't understand. The sage perhaps. But I? It is day again, at least what passes for such here. I must have fallen asleep after a brief bout of discouragement, such as I have not experienced for a long time. For why be discouraged, one of the thieves was saved, that is a generous percentage. I see the stick on the floor, not far from the bed. That is to say I see part of it, as of all one sees. It might just as well be at the equator, or one of the poles. No, not quite, for perhaps I shall devise a way of retrieving it, I am so ingenious. All is not then yet quite irrevocably lost. In the meantime nothing is mine any more, according to my definition, if I remember rightly, except my exercise-book, my lead and the French pencil, assuming it really exists. I did well to stop my inventory, it was a happy thought. I feel less weak, perhaps they fed me while I slept. I see the pot, the one that is not full, it is lost to me too. I shall doubtless be obliged to forget myself in the bed, as when I was a baby. At least I shall not be skelped. But enough about me. You would think I was relieved to be without my stick. I think I know how I might retrieve it. But something occurs to me. Are they depriving me of soup on purpose to help me die? One judges people too hastily. But in that case why feed me during my sleep? But there is no proof they have. But if they wished to help me would it not be more intelligent to give me poisoned soup, large quantities of poisoned soup? Perhaps they fear an autopsy. It is obvious they see a long way ahead. That reminds me that among my possessions I once had a little phial, unlabelled, containing pills. Laxatives? Sedatives? I forget. To turn to them for calm and merely obtain a diarrhoea, my, that would be annoying. In any case the question does not arise I am calm, insufficiently, I still lack a little calm. But enough about me. I'll see if there is anything in my little idea, I mean how to retrieve my stick. The fact is I must be very weak. If there is, anything in it I mean, I shall try and get myself out of the bed, for a start. If not I do not know what I shall do. Go and see how Macmann is getting on perhaps. I have always that resource. Why this need of activity? I am growing nervous.

One day, much later, to judge by his appearance, Macmann came to again, once again, in a kind of asylum. At first he did not know it was one, being plunged within it, but he was told so as soon as he was in a condition to receive news. They said in substance, You are now in the House of Saint John of God, with the number one hundred and sixty-six. Fear nothing, you are among friends. Friends! Well well. Take no thought for anything, it is we shall think and act for you, from now forward. We like it. Do not thank us therefore. In addition to the nourishment carefully calculated to keep you alive, and even well, you will receive, every Saturday, in honour of our patron, an imperial half-pint of porter and a plug of tobacco. Then followed instructions regarding his duties and prerogatives, for he was credited with a certain number of prerogatives, notwithstanding the bounties showered upon him. Stunned by this torrent of civility, for he had eluded charity all his days, Macmann did not immediately grasp that he was being spoken to. The room, or cell, in which he lay, was thronged with men and women dressed in white. They swarmed about his bed, those in the rear rising on tiptoe and craning their necks to get a better view of him. The speaker was a man, naturally, in the flower and the prime of life, his features stamped with mildness and severity in equal proportions, and he wore a scraggy beard no doubt intended to heighten his resemblance to the Messiah. To tell the truth, yet again, he did not so much read as improvise, or recite, to judge by the paper he held in his hand and on which from time to time he cast an anxious eye. He finally handed this paper to Macmann, together with the stump of an indelible pencil, the point of which he first wetted with his lips, and requested him to sign, adding that it was a mere formality. And when Macmann had obeyed, either because he was afraid of being punished if he refused or because he did not realize the seriousness of what he was doing, the other took back the paper, examined it and said, Mac what? It was then a woman's voice, extraordinarily shrill and unpleasant, was heard to say, Mann, his name is Macmann. This woman was standing behind him, so that he could not see her, and in each hand she clutched a bar of the bed. Who are you? said the speaker. Someone replied, But it is Moll, can't you see, her name is Moll. The speaker turned towards this informant, glared at him for a moment, then dropped his eyes. To be sure, he said, to be sure, I am out of sorts. He added, after a pause, Nice name, without its being quite clear whether this little tribute was aimed at the nice name of Moll or at the nice name of Macmann. Don't push, for Jesus sake! he said, irritably. Then, suddenly turning, he cried, What in God's name are you all pushing for for Christ sake? And indeed the room was filling more and more, under the influx of fresh spectators. Personally I'm going, said the speaker. Then all retreated, in great jostle and disorder, each one striving to be first out through the door, with the sole exception of Moll, who did not stir. But when all were gone she went to the door and shut it, then came back and sat down on a chair by the bed. She was a little old woman, immoderately ill-favored of both face and body. She seems called on to play a certain part in the remarkable events which, I hope, will enable me to make an end. The thin yellow arms contorted by some kind of bone deformation, the lips so broad and thick that they seemed to devour half the face, were at first sight her most revolting features. She wore by way of ear-rings two long ivory crucifixes which swayed wildly at the least movement of her head.

I pause to record that I feel in extraordinary form. Delirium perhaps.

It seemed probable to Macmann that he was committed to the care and charge of this person. Correct. For it had been decreed, by those in authority, that one hundred and sixty-six was Moll's, she having applied for him, formally. She brought him food (one large dish daily, to eat first hot, then cold), emptied his chamber-pot every morning first thing and showed him how to wash himself, his face and hands every day, and the other parts of the body successively in the course of the week, Monday the feet, Tuesday the legs up to the knees, Wednesday the thighs, and so on, culminating on Sunday with the neck and ears, no, Sunday he rested from washing. She swept the floor, shook up the bed from time to time and seemed to take an extreme pleasure in polishing until they shone the frosted lights of the unique window, which was never opened. She informed Macmann, when he did something, if that thing was permitted or not, and similarly, when he remained inert, whether or not he was entitled to. Does this mean that she stayed with him all the time? Why no, and no doubt she had other attentions to bestow elsewhere, and other instructions to give. But in the early stages, before he had grown used to this new tide in his fortune, she assuredly left him alone as little as possible and even watched over him part of the night. How understanding she was, and how good-natured, appears from the following anecdote. One day, not long after his admission, Macmann realized he was wearing, instead of his usual accoutrement, a long loose smock of coarse linen, or possibly drugget. He at once began to clamour loudly for his clothes, including probably the contents of his pockets, for he cried, My things! My things!, over and over again, tossing about in the bed and beating the blanket with his palms. Then Moll sat down on the edge of the bed and distributed her hands as follows, one on top of one of Macmann's, the other on his brow. She was so small that her feet did not reach to the floor. When he was a little calmer she told him that his clothes had certainly ceased to exist and could not therefore be returned to him. With regard to the objects found in the pockets, they had been assessed as quite worthless and fit only to be thrown away with the exception of a little silver knife-rest which he could have back at any time. But these declarations so distressed him that she hastened to add, with a laugh, that she was only joking and that in reality his clothes, cleaned, pressed, mended, strewn with mothballs and folded away in a cardboard box bearing his name and number, were as safe as if they had been received in deposit by the Bank of England. But as Macmann continued vehemently to demand his things, as if he did not understand a word of what she had just told him, she was obliged to invoke the regulations which tolerated on no account that an inmate should resume contact with the trappings of his derelict days until such time as he might be discharged. But as Macmann continued passionately to clamour for his things, and notably for his hat, she left him, saying he was not reasonable. And she came back a little later, holding with the tips of her fingers the hat in question, retrieved perhaps from the rubbish-heap at the end of the vegetable-garden, for to know everything takes too long, for it was fringed with manure and seemed to be rotting away. And what is more she suffered him to put it on, and even helped him to do so, helping him to sit up in the bed and arranging his pillows in such a way that he might remain propped up without fatigue. And she contemplated with tenderness the old bewildered face relaxing, and in its tod of hair the mouth trying to smile, and the little red eyes turning timidly towards her as if in gratitude or rolling towards the recovered hat, and the hands raised to set it on more firmly and returning to rest trembling on the blanket. And at last a long look passed between them and Moll's lips puffed and parted in a dreadful smile, which made Macmann's eyes waver like those of an animal glared on by its master and compelled then finally to look away. End of anecdote. This must be the selfsame hat that was abandoned in the middle of the plain, its resemblance to it is so great, allowance being made for the additional wear and tear. Can it be then that it is not the same Macmann at all, after all, in spite of the great resemblance (for those who know the power of the passing years), both physical and otherwise. It is true the Macmanns are legion in the island and pride themselves, what is more, with few exceptions, on having one and all, in the last analysis, sprung from the same illustrious ball. It is therefore inevitable they should resemble one another, now and then, to the point of being confused even in the minds of those who wish them well and would like nothing better than to tell between them. No matter, any old remains of flesh and spirit do, there is no sense in stalking people. So long as it is what is called a living being you can't go wrong, you have the guilty one. For a long time he did not stir from his bed, not knowing if he could walk, or even stand, and fearing to run foul of the authorities, if he could. Let us then first consider this first phase of Macmann's stay in the House of Saint John of God. We shall then pass on to the second, and even to the third, if necessary.

A thousand little things to report, very strange, in view of my situation, if I interpret them correctly. But my notes have a curious tendency, as I realize at last, to annihilate all they purport to record. So I hasten to turn aside from this extraordinary heat, to mention only it, which has seized on certain parts of my economy, I will not specify which. And to think I was expecting rather to grow cold, if anything!

This first phase, that of the bed, was characterized by the evolution of the relationship between Macmann and his keeper.

There sprang up gradually between them a kind of intimacy which, at a given moment, led them to lie together and copulate as best they could. For given their age and scant experience of carnal love, it was only natural they should not succeed, at the first shot, in giving each other the impression they were made for each other. The spectacle was then offered of Macmann trying to bundle his sex into his partner's like a pillow into a pillow-slip, folding it in two and stuffing it in with his fingers. But far from losing heart they warmed to their work. And though both were completely impotent they finally succeeded, summoning to their aid all the resources of the skin, the mucus and the imagination, in striking from their dry and feeble clips a kind of sombre gratification. So that Moll exclaimed, being (at that stage) the more expansive of the two, Oh would we had but met sixty years ago! But on the long road to this what flutterings, alarms and bashful fumblings, of which only this, that they gave Macmann some insight into the meaning of the expression, Two is company. He then made unquestionable progress in the use of the spoken word and learnt in a short time to let fall, at the right time, the yesses, noes, mores and enoughs that keep love alive. It was also the occasion of his penetrating into the enchanted world of reading, thanks to the inflammatory letters which Moll brought and put into his hands. And the memories of school are so tenacious, for those who have been there, that he was soon able to dispense with the explanations of his correspondent and understand all unaided, holding the sheet of paper as far from his eyes as his arms permitted. While he read Moll held a little aloof, with downcast eyes, saying to herself, Now he's at the part where, and a little later, Now he's at the part where, and so remained until the rustle of the sheet going back into the envelope announced that he had finished. Then she turned eagerly towards him, in time to see him raise the letter to his lips or press it against his heart, another reminiscence of the fourth form. Then he gave it back to her and she put it under his pillow with the others there already, arranged in chronological order and tied together by a favor. These letters did not much vary in form and tenor, which greatly facilitated matters for Macmann. Example. Sweetheart, Not one day goes by that I do not give thanks to God, on my bended knees, for having found you, before I die. For we shall soon die, you and I, that is obvious. That it may be at the same moment exactly is all I ask. In any case I have the key of the medicine cupboard. But let us profit first by this superb sundown, after the long day of storm. Are you not of this opinion? Sweetheart! Ah would we had met but seventy years ago! No, all is for the best, we shall not have time to grow to loathe each other, to see our youth slip by, to recall with nausea the ancient rapture, to seek in the company of third parties, you on the one hand, I on the other, that which together we can no longer compass, in a word to get to know each other. One must look things in the face, must one not, sweet pet? When you hold me in your arms, and I you in mine, it naturally does not amount to much, compared to the transports of youth, and even middle age. But all is relative, let us bear that in mind, stags and hinds have their needs and we have ours. It is even astonishing that you manage so well, I can hardly get over it, what a chaste and sober life you must have led. I too, you must have noticed it. Consider moreover that the flesh is not the end-all and the be-all, especially at our age, and name me the lovers who can do with their eyes what we can do with ours, which will soon have seen all there is for them to see and have often great difficulty in remaining open, and with their tenderness, without the help of passion, what by this means alone we realize daily, when separated by our respective obligations. Consider furthermore, since there is nothing more for us to hide, that I was never beautiful or well-proportioned, but ugly and even misshapen, to judge by the testimonies I have received. Papa notably used to say that people would run a mile from me, I have not forgotten the expression. And you, sweet, even when you were of an age to quicken the pulse of beauty, did you exhibit the other requisites? I doubt it. But with the passing of the years we have become scarcely less hideous than even our best favored contemporaries and you, in particular, have kept your hair. And thanks to our having never served, never understood, we are not without freshness and innocence, it seems to me. Moral, for us at last it is the season of love, let us make the most of it, there are pears that only ripen in December. Do not fret about our methods, leave all that to me, and I warrant you we'll surprise each other yet. With regard to tetty-beshy I must beg to differ, it is well worth persevering with, in my opinion. Follow my instructions, you'll come back for more. For shame, you dirty old man! It's all these bones that makes it awkward, that I grant you. Well, we must just accept ourselves as we are. And above all *not fret,* these are trifles. Let us think of the hours when, spent, we lie twined together in the dark, our hearts laboring as one, and listen to the wind saying what it is to be abroad, at night, in winter, and what it is to have been what we have been, and sink together, in an unhappiness that has no name. That is how we must look at things. So courage, my sweet old hairy Mac, and oyster kisses just where you think from your own Sucky Moll. P.S. I enquired about the oysters, I have hopes. Such was the rather rambling style of the declarations which Moll, despairing no doubt of giving vent to her feelings by the normal channels, addressed three or four times a week to Macmann, who never answered, I mean in writing, but manifested by every other means in his power how pleased he was to receive them. But towards the close of this idyll, that is to say when it was too late, he began to compose brief rimes of curious structure, to offer to his mistress, for he felt she was drifting away from him. Example.

Hairy Mac and Sucky Molly
In the ending days and nights
Of unending melancholy
Love it is at last unites.

Other example.

G

To the lifelong promised land
Of the nearest cemetery
With his Sucky hand in hand
Love it is at last leads Hairy.

He had time to compose ten or twelve more or less in this vein, all remarkable for their exaltation of love regarded as a kind of lethal glue, a conception frequently to be met with in mystic texts. And it is extraordinary that Macmann should have succeeded, in so short a time and after such inauspicious beginnings, in elevating himself to a view of this altitude. And one can only speculate on what he might have achieved if he had become acquainted with true sexuality at a less advanced age.

I am lost. Not a word.

Inauspicious beginnings indeed, during which his feeling for Moll was frankly one of repugnance. Her lips in particular repelled him, those selfsame lips, or so little changed as to make no matter, that some months later he was to suck with grunts of pleasure, so that at the very sight of them he not only closed his eyes, but covered them with his hands for greater safety. She it was therefore who at this period exerted herself in tireless ardours, which may serve to explain why she seemed to weaken in the end and stand in her turn in need of stimulation. Unless it was simply a question of health. Which does not exclude a third hypothesis, namely that Moll, having finally decided that she had been mistaken in Macmann and that he was not the man she had taken him for, sought a means of putting an end to their intercourse, but gently, in order not to give him a shock. Unfortunately our concern here is not with Moll, who after all is only a female, but with Macmann, and not with the close of their relations, but rather with the beginning. Of the brief period of plenitude between these two extremes, when between the warming up of the one party and the cooling down of the other there was established a fleeting equality of temperature, no further mention will be made. For if it is indispensable to have in order not to have had and in order to have no longer, there is no obligation to expatiate upon it. But let us rather let events speak for themselves, that is more or less the right tone. Example. One day, just as Macmann was getting used to being loved, though without as yet responding as he was subsequently to do, he thrust Moll's face away from his on the pretext of examining her ear-rings. But as she made to return to the charge he checked her again with the first words that came into his head, namely; Why two Christs?, implying that in his opinion one was more than sufficient. To which she made the absurd reply, Why two ears? But she obtained his forgiveness a moment later, saying, with a smile (she smiled at the least thing), Besides they are the thieves, Christ is in my mouth. Then parting her jaws and pulling down her blobber-lip she discovered, breaking with its solitary fang the monotomy of the gums, a long yellow canine bared to the roots and carved, with the drill probably, to represent the celebrated sacrifice. With the forefinger of her free hand she fingered it. It's loose, she said, one of these fine mornings I'll wake up and find I've swallowed it, perhaps I should have it out. She let go her lip, which sprang back into place with a smack. This incident made a strong impression on Macmann and Moll rose with a bound in his affections. And in the pleasure he was later to enjoy, when he put his tongue in her mouth and let it wander over her gums, this rotten crucifix had assuredly its part. But from these harmless aids what love is free? Sometimes it is an object, a garter I believe or a sweat-absorber for the armpit. And sometimes it is the simple image of a third party. A few words in conclusion on the decline of this liaison. No, I can't.

Weary with my weariness, white last moon, sole regret, not even. To be dead, before her, on her, with her, and turn, dead on dead, about poor mankind, and never have to die any more, from among the living. Not even, not even that. My moon was here below, far below, the little I was able to desire. And one day, soon, soon, one earthlit night, beneath the earth, a dying being will say, like me, in the earthlight, Not even, not even that, and die, without having been able to find a regret.

Moll. I'm going to kill her. She continued to look after Macmann, but she was no longer the same. When she had finished cleaning up she sat down on a chair, in the middle of the room, and remained without stirring. If he called her she went and perched on the edge of the bed and even submitted to be titillated. But it was obvious her thoughts were elsewhere and her only wish to return to her chair and resume the now familiar gesture of massaging her stomach, slowly, weighing on it with her two hands. She was also beginning to smell. She had never smelt sweet, but between not smelling sweet and giving off the smell she was giving off now there is a gulf. She was also subject to fits of vomiting. Turning away, so that her lover should only see her convulsive back, she vomited at length on the floor. And these dejections remained sometimes for hours where they fell, until such time as she had the strength to go and fetch what was needed to clean up the mess. Half a century younger she might have been taken for pregnant. At the same time her hair began to fall out in abundance and she confessed to Macmann that she did not dare comb it any more, for fear of making it fall out even faster. He said to himself with satisfaction, She tells me everything. But these were small things compared to the change in her complexion, now rapidly turning from yellow to saffron. The sight of her so diminished did not damp Macmann's desire to take her, all stinking, yellow, bald and vomiting, in his arms. And he would certainly have done so had she not been opposed to it. One can understand him (her too). For when one has within reach the one and only love requited of a life so monstrously prolonged, it is natural one should wish to profit by it, before it is too late, and refuse to be deterred by feelings of squeamishness excusable in the faint-hearted, but which true love disdains. And though all pointed to Moll's being out of sorts, Macmann could not help interpreting her attitude as a falling off of her affection for him. And perhaps indeed there was something of that too. At all events the more she declined the more Macmann longed to crush her to his breast, which is at least sufficiently curious and unusual to deserve of mention. And when she turned and looked at him (and from time to time she did so still), with eyes in which he fancied he could read boundless regret and love, then a kind of frenzy seized upon him and he began to belabor with his fists his chest, his head and even the mattress, writhing and crying out, in the hope perhaps she would take pity on him and come and comfort him and dry his tears, as on the day when he had demanded his hat. No, it was not that, it was without malice he cried, writhed and beat his breast, for she made no attempt to stop him and even left the room if it went on too long for her liking. Then, all alone and unobserved, he continued to behave as if beside himself, which is proof positive, is it not, that he was disinterested, unless of course he suspected her of having stopped outside the door to listen. And when he grew calm again at last he mourned the long immunity he had lost, from shelter, charity and human tenderness. And he even carried his inconsequence to the length of wondering what right anyone had to take care of him. In a word most evil days, for Macmann. For Moll too probably, naturally, admittedly. It was at this time she lost her tooth. It fell unaided from the socket, happily in the daytime, so that she was able to recover it and put it away in a safe place. Macmann said to himself, when she told him, There was a time she would have made me a present of it, or at least shown it to me. But a little later he said, firstly, To have told me, when she need not have, is a mark of confidence and affection, and secondly, But I would have known in any case, when she opened her mouth to speak or smile, and finally, But she does not speak or smile any more. One morning early a man whom he had never seen came and told him that Moll was dead. There's one out of the way at least. My name is Lemuel, he said, though my parents were probably Aryan, and

it is in my charge you are from now on. Here is your porridge.
Eat while it is boiling.

A last effort. Lemuel gave the impression of being slightly
more stupid than malevolent, and yet his malevolence was considerable. When Macmann, more and more disturbed by his
situation apparently and what is more now capable of isolating
and expressing well enough to be understood a little of the little
that passed through his mind, when Macmann I say asked a
question it was seldom he got an immediate answer. When asked
for example to state whether Saint John of Gods was a private
institution or run by the State, a hospice for the aged and infirm
or a madhouse, if once in one might entertain the hope of one
day getting out and, in the affirmative, by means of what steps,
Lemuel remained for a long time plunged in thought, sometimes for as long as ten minutes or a quarter of an hour, motionless or if you prefer scratching his head or his armpit, as if
such questions had never crossed his mind, or possibly thinking
about something quite different. And if Macmann, growing
impatient or perhaps feeling he had not made himself clear,
ventured to try again, an imperious gesture bid him be silent.
Such was this Lemuel, viewed from a certain angle. Or he cried,
stamping the ground with indescribable nervousness, Let me
think, you shite! It usually ended by his saying he did not
know. But he was subject to almost hypomaniacal fits of good-
humor. Then he would add, But I'll enquire. And taking out a
note-book as fat as a ship's log he made note, murmuring, Private
or state, mad or like me, how out, etc. Macmann could then be
sure he would never hear any more about it. May I get up?
he said one day. Already in Moll's lifetime he had expressed
the wish to get up and go out into the fresh air, but timidly,
as when one asks for the moon. And he had then been told that
if he was good he might indeed be let up one day, and out into
the pure plateau air, and that on that day, in the great hall
where the staff assembled at dawn before entering on their
duties, there would be seen pinned on the board a note thus

96

conceived, Let one hundred and sixty-six get up and go out. For when it came to the regulations Moll was inflexible and their voice was stronger than the voice of love, in her heart, whenever they made themselves heard there simultaneously. The oysters for example, which the Board had refused in a note calling her attention to the article whereby they were prohibited, but which she could easily have smuggled in, Macmann never saw sight or sign of the oysters. But Lemuel was made of sterner stuff, in this connexion, and far from being a stickler for the statutes seemed to have little or no acquaintance with them. Indeed the question might have arisen, in the mind of one looking down upon the scene, as to whether he had all his wits about him. For when not rooted to the spot in a daze he was to be seen, with heavy, furious, reeling tread, stamping up and down for hours on end, gesticulating and ejaculating unintelligible words. Flayed alive by memory, his mind crawling with cobras, not daring to dream or think and powerless not to, his cries were of two kinds, those having no other cause than moral anguish and those, similar in every respect, by means of which he hoped to forestall same. Physical pain, on the contrary, seemed to help him greatly. And one day rolling up the leg of his trousers, he showed Macmann his shin covered with bruises, scars and abrasions. Then producing smartly a hammer from an inner pocket he dealt himself, right in the middle of his ancient wounds, so violent a blow that he fell down backwards, or perhaps I should say forwards. But the part he struck most readily, with his hammer, was the head, and that is understandable, for it too is a bony part, and sensitive, and difficult to miss, and the seat of all the shit and misery, so you rain blows upon it, with more pleasure than on the leg for example, which never did you any harm, it's only human. Up! cried Macmann. Let me up! Lemuel came to a standstill. What? he roared. Up! cried Macmann. Let me up! Let me up!

I have had a visit. Things were going too well. I had forgotten myself, lost myself. I exaggerate. Things were not going

too badly. I was elsewhere. Another was suffering. Then I had
the visit. To bring me back to dying. If that amuses them. The
fact is they don't know, neither do I, but they think they know.
An aeroplane passes, flying low, with a noise like thunder. It
is a noise quite unlike thunder, one says thunder but one does
not think it, it is just a loud, fleeting noise, nothing more, unlike any other. It is certainly the first time I have heard it here,
to my knowledge. But I have heard aeroplanes elsewhere and
have even seen them in flight, I saw the very first in flight and
then in the end the latest models, oh not the very latest, the
very second-latest, the very antepenultimate. I was present at
one of the first loopings of the loop, so help me God. I was not
afraid. It was above a racecourse, my mother held me by the
hand. She kept saying, It's a miracle, a miracle. Then I changed
my mind. We were not often of the same mind. One day we were
walking along the road, up a hill of extraordinary steepness,
near home I imagine, my memory is full of steep hills, I get
them confused. I said, The sky is further away than you think, is
it not, mama? It was without malice, I was simply thinking of all
the leagues that separated me from it. She replied, to me her son,
It is precisely as far away as it appears to be. She was right.
But at the time I was aghast. I can still see the spot, opposite
Tyler's gate. A market-gardener, he had only one eye and wore
side-whiskers. That's the idea, rattle on. You could see the sea,
the islands, the headlands, the isthmuses, the coast stretching
away to north and south and the crooked moles of the harbor.
We were on our way home from the butcher's. My mother? Perhaps it is just another story, told me by some one who found it
funny. The stories I was told, at one time! And all funny, not
one not funny. In any case here I am back in the shit. The
aeroplane, on the other hand, has just passed over at two hundred miles an hour perhaps. It's a good speed, for the present
day. I am with it in spirit, naturally. All the things I was always
with in spirit. In body no. Not such a fool. Here is the programme anyhow, the end of the programme. They think they can
confuse me and make me lose sight of my programmes. Proper

cunts whoever they are. Here it is. Visit, various remarks, Macmann continued, agony recalled, Macmann continued, then mixture of Macmann and agony as long as possible. It does not depend on me, my lead is not inexhaustible, nor my exercise-book, nor Macmann, nor myself in spite of appearances. That all may be wiped out at the same instant is all I ask, for the moment. The visit. I felt a violent blow on the head. He had perhaps been there for some time. One does not care to be kept waiting for ever, one draws attention to oneself as best one can, it's human. I don't doubt he gave me due warning, before he hit me. I don't know what he wanted. He's gone now. What an idea, all the same, to hit me on the head. The light has been queer ever since, oh I insinuate nothing, dim and at the same time radiant, perhaps I have concussion. His mouth opened, his lips worked, but I heard nothing. He might just as well have said nothing. And yet I am not deaf, witness the aeroplane, if I hear nothing it is because there is nothing to hear. But perhaps life has dulled my irritability to specifically human sounds. I myself for example make no sound, well well, can't go back on it now, no, not the tiniest. And yet I pant, cough, moan and gulp right up against my ear, I could swear to it. In other words I do not know to what I owe the honor. He seemed vexed. Must I describe him? Why not? He may be important. I had a clear view of him. Black suit of antiquated cut, or perhaps come back into the fashion, black tie, snow-white shirt, heavily starched clown's cuffs almost entirely covering the hands, oily black hair, a long, dismal, glabrous, floury face, sombre lacklustre eyes, medium height and build, block-hat pressed delicately to stomach with finger-tips, then without warning in a gesture of extraordinary suddenness and precision slapped on skull. A folding-rule, together with a fin of white handkerchief, emerged from the breast pocket. I took him at first for the undertaker's man, annoyed at having called prematurely. He remained some time, seven hours at least. Perhaps he hoped to have the satisfaction of seeing me expire before he left, that would probably have saved him time and trouble. For a moment I thought he was going to finish me off. What a hope, it would have been a crime. He must have left at six o'clock, his working day ended. The light is queer ever since. That it to say he went a first time, came back some hours later, then left for good. He must have been here from nine to twelve, then from two to six, now I have it. He kept looking at his watch, a turnip. Perhaps he will come back to-morrow. It was in the morning he hit me, about ten o'clock probably. In the afternoon he did not touch me, though I did not see him immediately, he was already in position when I saw him, standing beside the bed. I speak of morning and afternoon and of such and such an hour, if you simply must speak of people you simply must put yourself in their place, it is not difficult. The only thing you must never speak of is your happiness, I can think of nothing else for the moment. Better even not to think of it. Standing by the bed he watched me. Seeing my lips move, for I tried to speak, he stooped down to me. I had things to ask him, to give me my stick for example. He would have refused. Then with clasped hands and tears in my eyes I would have begged it of him as a favor. This humiliation has been denied to me thanks to my aphony. My voice has gone dead, the rest will follow. I could have written, on a page of my exercise-book, and shown to him, Please give me back my stick, or, Be so kind as to hand me up my stick. But I had hidden the exercise-book under the blanket, so that he might not take it from me. I did so without thinking that he had been there for some time (otherwise he would not have struck me) watching me writing, for I must have been writing when he came, and that consequently he could easily have taken my exercise-book if he had wished, and without thinking either that he was watching me when I slipped it out of sight, and that consequently the only effect of my precaution was to draw his attention to the very object I wished to hide from him. There's reasoning for you. For of all I ever had in this world all has been taken from me, except the exercise-book, so I cherish it, it's human. The lead too, I was forgetting the lead, but what is a lead, without paper? He must have said to himself, over his lunch, This afternoon I'll take his exercise-book from him, he seems to cherish it. But when he came back from his lunch the exercise-book was no longer in the place where he had seen me put it, he had not thought of that. His umbrella, have I mentioned his umbrella, the tightest rolled I ever saw? Shifting it every few minutes from one hand to the other he leaned his weight upon it, standing beside the bed. Then it bent. He made use of it to raise my blankets. It was with this umbrella that I thought he was going to kill me, with its long sharp point, he had only to plunge it in my heart. Wilful murder, people would have said. Perhaps he will come back to-morrow, better equipped, or with an assistant, now that he is familiar with the premises. But if he watched me I too watched him, I think we gazed at each other literally for hours, without winking. He probably imagined he could stare me down, because I am old and helpless. The poor bastard. It was so long since I had seen a biped of this description that I had my eyes out on stalks, as the saying is, for fear of not being able to credit them. I said to myself, One of these days they'll start grazing the trees. And the face they have! I had forgotten. At a certain moment, incommoded by the smell probably, he squeezed himself in between the bed and the wall, to try and open the window. He couldn't. In the morning I didn't take my eyes off him. But in the afternoon I slept a little. I don't know what he did while I was asleep, rummaged in my possessions probably, with his umbrella, they are scattered all over the floor now. I thought for a moment he had been sent by the funeral people. Those who have enabled me to live till now will no doubt see to it that I am buried with a minimum of ceremony. Here lies Malone at last, with the dates to give a faint idea of the time he took to be excused and then to distinguish him from his namesakes, numerous in the island and beyond the grave. Funny I never ran into one, to my knowledge, not one. There is still time. Here lies a ne'er-do-well, six feet under hell. But for a moment only, I mean half-an-hour at most. Then I tried him with other functions, all equally disappointing. Strange need to know who people are and what they do for a living and what they want with you. In spite of the ease with which he wore his black and manipulated his umbrella and his consummate mastery of the block-hat, I had for a time the impression he was disguised, but from what if I may say so, and as what? At a given moment, yet another, he took fright, for his breath came faster and he moved away from the bed. It was then I saw he was wearing brown boots, which gave me such a shock as no words can convey. They were copiously caked with fresh mud and I said to myself, Through what sloughs has he had to toil to reach me? I wonder if he was looking for something in particular, it would be so nice to know. I shall tear a page out of my exercise-book and reproduce upon it, from memory, what follows, and show it to him to-morrow, or to-day, or some other day, if he ever comes back. 1. Who are you? 2. What do you do, for a living? 3. Are you looking for something in particular? What else? 4. Why are you so cross? 5. Have I offended you? 6. Do you know anything about me? 7. It was wrong of you to strike me. 8. Give me my stick. 9. Are you your own employer? 10. If not who sends you? 11. Put back my things where you found them. 12. Why has my soup been stopped? 13. For what reason are my pots no longer emtied? 14. Do you think I shall last much longer? 15. May I ask you a favor? 16. Your conditions are mine. 17. Why brown boots and whence the mud? 18. You couldn't by any chance let me have the butt of a pencil? 19. Number your answers. 20. Don't go, I haven't finished. Will one page suffice? There cannot be many left. I might as well ask for a rubber while I am about it. 21. Could you lend me an India rubber? When he had gone I said to myself, But surely I have seen him somewhere before. And the people I have seen have seen me too, I can guarantee that. But of whom may it not be said, I know that man? Drivel, drivel. And then at evening morning is so far away. I had stopped looking at him. I had got used to him. I was thinking of him, trying to understand, you can't do that and look at the same time. I did not even see him go. Oh he did not vanish, after the fashion of a ghost, no, I heard him, the clank when he took out his watch, the satisfied thump of the umbrella on the floor, the rightabout, the rapid steps towards the door, its soft closing and finally, I am sorry to say, a gay and lively whistle dying away. What have I omitted? Little things, nothings. They will come back to me later, make me see more clearly what has happened and say, Ah if I had only known then, now it is too late. Yes, little by little I shall see him as he just has been, or as he should have been for me to be able to say, yet again, Too late, too late. There's feeling for you. Or he is perhaps just the first of a series of visitors, all different. They are going to relay one another, and they are numerous. To-morrow perhaps he will be wearing leggings, riding-breeches and a check cap, with a whip in his hand to make up for the umbrella and a horse-shoe in his button-hole. All the people I have ever caught a glimpse of, at close quarters or at a distance, may file past from now on, that is obvious. There may even be women and children, I have caught a glimpse of a few, they will all be armed with something to lean on and rummage in my things with, they will all give me a clout on the head to begin with and then spend the rest of the day glaring at me in anger and disgust. I shall have to revise my questionnaire so as to adapt it to all and sundry. Perhaps one, one day, unmindful of his instructions, will give me my stick. Or I might be able to catch one, a little girl for example, and half strangle her, three quarters, until she promises to give me my stick, give me soup, empty my pots, kiss me, fondle me, smile to me, give me my hat, stay with me, follow the hearse weeping into her handkerchief, that would be nice. I am such a good man, at bottom, such a good man, how is it nobody ever noticed it? A little girl would be into my barrow, she would undress before me, sleep beside me, have nobody but me, I would jam the bed against the door to prevent her running away, but then she would throw herself out of the window, when they got to know she was with me they would bring soup for two, I would teach her love and loathing, she would never forget me, I would die delighted, she would close my eyes and put a plug in my arse-hole, as per instructions. Easy, Malone, take

103

it easy, you old whore. That reminds me, how long can one fast with impunity? The Lord Mayor of Cork lasted for ages, but he was young, and then he had political convictions, human ones too probably, just plain human convictions. And he allowed himself a sip of water from time to time, sweetened probably. Water, for pity's sake! How is it I am not thirsty. There must be drinking going on inside me, my secretions. Yes, let us talk a little about me, that will be a rest from all these blackguards. What light! Foretaste of paradise? My head. On fire, full of boiling oil. What shall I die of, in the end? A transport of blood to the brain? That would be the last straw. The pain is almost unbearable, upon my soul it is. Incandescent migraine. Death must take me for someone else. It's the heart's fault, as in the bosom of the match king, Schneider, Schroeder, I forget. It too is burning, with shame, of itself, of me, of them, shame of everything, except of beating apparently. It's nothing, mere nervousness. And who knows, perhaps the first to fail will be my breath, after all. After each avowal, before and during, what swirling murmurs. The window says break of day, rack of tattered rainclouds stampeding. Have a nice time. Far from this molten gloom. Yes, my last gasps are not what they might be, the bellows won't go down, the air is choking me, perhaps it is a little lacking in oxygen. Macmann pygmy beneath the great black gesticulating pines gazes at the distant raging sea. The others are there too, or at their windows, like me, but on their feet, they must be able to move, or to be moved, no, not like me, they can't do anything for anybody, clinging to the shivering poplars, or at their windows, listening. But perhaps I should finish with myself first, in so far naturally as such a thing is possible. The speed I am turning at now makes things difficult admittedly, but it probably can only increase, that is the thing to be considered. Mem, add to the questionnaire, If you happen to have a match try and light it. How is it I heard nothing when he spoke to me and yet heard him leave, whistling? Perhaps he only feigned to speak to me, to try and make me think I had gone deaf. Do I hear anything at the present instant? Let me see. No, the answer is no. Neither the wind, nor the sea, nor the paper, nor the air I exhale with such labor. But this innumerable babble, like a multitude whispering? I don't understand. With my distant hand I count the pages that remain. They will do. This exercise-book is my life, this big child's exercise-book, it has taken me a long time to resign myself to that. And yet I shall not throw it away. For I want to put down in it, for the last time, those I have called to my help, but ill, so that they did not understand, so that they may cease with me. Now rest.

Wearing over his long shirt a great striped cloak reaching down to his ankles Macmann took the air in all weathers, from morning to night. And more than once they had been obliged to go out looking for him with lanterns, to bring him back to his cell, for he had remained deaf to the call of the bell and to the shouts and threats first of Lemuel, then of the other keepers. Then the keepers, in their white clothes, armed with sticks and lanterns, spread out from the buildings and beat the thickets, the copses and the fern-brakes, calling the fugitive by name and threatening him with the direst reprisals if he did not surrender immediately. But they finally remarked that he hid, when he did, always in the same place and that such a deployment of force was unnecessary. From then on it was Lemuel who went out alone, in silence, as always when he knew what he had to do, straight to the bush in which Macmann had made his lair, whenever this was necessary. My God. And often the two of them remained there for some time, in the bush, before going in, huddled together, for the lair was small, saying nothing, perhaps listening to the noises of the night, the owls, the wind in the leaves, the sea when it was high enough to make its voice heard, and then the other night sounds that you cannot tell the meaning of. And it sometimes happened that Macmann, weary of not being alone went away alone and back into his cell and remained there until Lemuel rejoined him, much later. It was a genuine English park, though far from England, extravagantly

unformal, luxuriant to the point of wildness, the trees at war
with one another, and the bushes, and the wild flowers and
weeds, all ravening for earth and light. One evening Macmann
went back to his cell with a branch torn from a dead bramble,
for use as a stick to support him as he walked. Then Lemuel
took it from him and struck him with it over and over again, no,
that won't work, then Lemuel called a keeper by the name of
Pat, a thorough brute though puny in appearance, and said to
him, Pat, will you look at that. Then Pat snatched the stick from
Macmann who, seeing the turn things were taking, was holding
it clutched tight in his two hands, and struck him with it until
Lemuel told him to stop, and even for some little time afterwards.
All this without a word of explanation. So that a little later
Macmann, having brought back from his walk a hyacinth he
had torn up bulb and roots in the hope of being able to keep it
a little longer thus than if he had simply plucked it, was fiercely
reprimanded by Lemuel who wrenched the pretty flower from
his hands and threatened to hand him over to Jack again, no,
to Pat again, Jack is a different one. And yet the fact of having
half demolished the bush, a kind of laurel, in order to hide in
it, had never brought upon his head the least reproof. This is
not necessarily surprising, there was no proof against him. Had
he been questioned about it he would naturally have told the
truth, for he did not suspect he had done anything wrong. But
they must have assumed he would do nothing but lie and stoutly
deny and that it was therefore useless to press him with questions. Besides no questions were ever asked in the House of
Saint John of God, but stern measures were simply taken, or
not taken, according to the dictates of a peculiar logic. For,
when you come to think of it, in virtue of what possible principle
of justice can a flower in the hand fasten on the bearer the crime
of having gathered it? Or was the mere fact of holding it for
all to see in itself a felony, analogous to that of the receiver or
fence? And if so would it not have been preferable to make this
known, quite plainly and frankly, to all concerned, so that the
sense of guilt, instead of merely following on the guilty act,

106

might precede and accompany it as well? Problem. But nicely posed, I think, very nicely indeed. Thanks to the white cloak with its blue butcher stripes no confusion was possible between the Macmanns on the one hand and the Lemuels, Pats and Jacks on the other. The birds. Numerous and varied in the dense foliage they lived without fear all the year round, or in fear only of their congeners, and those which in summer or in winter flew off to other climes came back the following winter or the following summer, roughly speaking. The air was filled with their voices, especially at dawn and dusk, and those which set off in flocks in the morning, such as the crows and starlings, for distant pastures, came back the same evening all joyous to the sanctuary, where their sentinels awaited them. The gulls were many in stormy weather which paused here on their flight inland. They wheeled long in the cruel air, screeching with anger, then settled in the grass or on the house-tops, mistrustful of the trees. But that is all beside the point, like so many things. All is pretext, Sapo and the birds, Moll, the peasants, those who in the towns seek one another out and fly from one another, my doubts which do not interest me, my situation, my possessions, pretext for not coming to the point, the abandoning, the raising of the arms and going down, without further splash, even though it may annoy the bathers. Yes, there is no good pretending, it is hard to leave everything. The horror-worn eyes linger abject on all they have beseeched so long, in a last prayer, the true prayer at last, the one that asks for nothing. And it is then a little breath of fulfilment revives the dead longings and a murmur is born in the silent world, reproaching you affectionately with having despaired too late. The last word in the way of viaticum. Let us try it another way. The pure plateau

Try and go on. The pure plateau air. Yes, it was a plateau, Moll had not lied, or rather a great mound with gentle slopes. The entire top was occupied by the domain of Saint John and there the wind blew almost without ceasing, causing the stoutest

H

trees to bend and groan, breaking the boughs, tossing the bushes, lashing the ferns to fury, flattening the grass and whirling leaves and flowers far away, I hope I have not forgotten anything. Good. A high wall encompassed it about, without however shutting off the view, unless you happened to be in its lee. How was this possible? Why thanks to the rising ground to be sure, culminating in a summit called the Rock, because of the rock that was on it. From here a fine view was to be obtained of the plain, the sea, the mountains, the smoke of the town and the buildings of the institution, bulking large in spite of their remoteness and all astir with little dots or flecks forever appearing and disappearing, in reality the keepers coming and going, perhaps mingled with I was going to say with the prisoners! For seen from this distance the striped cloak had no stripes, nor indeed any great resemblance to a cloak at all. So that one could only say, when the first shock of surprise was past, Those are men and women, you know, people, without being able to specify further. A stream at long intervals bestrid—but to hell with all this fucking scenery. Where could it have risen anyway, tell me that. Underground perhaps. In a word a little Paradise for those who like their nature sloven. Macmann sometimes wondered what was lacking to his happiness. The right to be abroad in all weathers morning, noon and night, trees and bushes with outstretched branches to wrap him round and hide him, food and lodging such as they were free of all charge, superb views on every hand out over the lifelong enemy, a minimum of persecution and corporal punishment, the song of the birds, no human contact except with Lemuel, who went out of his way to avoid him, the faculties of memory and reflection stunned by the incessant walking and high wind, Moll dead, what more could he wish? I must be happy, he said, it is less pleasant than I should have thought. And he clung closer and closer to the wall, but not too close, for it was guarded, seeking a way out into the desolation of having nobody and nothing, the wilds of the hunted, the scant bread and the scant shelter and the black joy of the solitary way, in helplessness and will-lessness, through all the beauty, the knowing and the loving. Which he stated by saying, for he was artless. I have had enough, without pausing a moment to reflect on what it was he had enough of or to compare it with what it had been he had had enough of, until he lost it, and would have enough of again, when he got it back again, and without suspecting that the thing so often felt to be excessive, and honored by such a variety of names, was perhaps in reality always one and the same. But there was one reflecting in his place and setting down coldly the sign of equality wh . : it was needed, as if that could make any difference. So he had only to go on gasping, in his artless way, Enough! Enough!, as he crept along by the wall under the cover of the bushes, searching for a breach through which he might slip out, under cover of night, or a place with footholds where he might climb over. But the wall was unbroken and smooth and topped uninterruptedly with broken glass, of a bottle green. But let us cast a glance at the main entrance, wide enough to admit two large vehicles abreast and flanked by two charming lodges covered with Virginia creeper and occupied by large deserving families, to judge by the swarms of little brats playing nearby, pursuing one another with cries of joy, rage and grief. But space hemmed him in on every side and held him in its toils, with the multitude of other faintly stirring, faintly struggling things, such as the children, the lodges and the gates, and like a sweat of things the moments streamed away in a great chaotic conflux of oozings and torrents, and the trapped huddled things changed and died each one according to its solitude. Beyond the gate, on the road, shapes passed that Macmann could not understand, because of the bars, because of all the trembling and raging behind him and beside him, because of the cries, the sky, the earth enjoining him to fall and his long blind life. A keeper came out of one of the lodges, in obedience to a telephone-call probably, all in white, a long black object in his hand, a key, and the children lined up along the drive. Suddenly there were women. All fell silent. The heavy gates swung open, driving the keeper before them. He backed away, then suddenly turned and fled to his doorstep. The road appeared, white with dust, bordered with dark masses, stretched a little way and ran up dead, against a narrow grey sky. Macmann let go the tree that hid him and turned back up the hill, not running, for he could hardly walk, but as fast as he could, bowed and stumbling, helping himself forward with the boles and boughs that offered. Little by little the haze formed again, and the sense of absence, and the captive things began to murmur again, each one to itself, and it was as if nothing had ever happened or would ever happen again.

Others besides Marmann strayed from morning to night, stooped under the heavy cloak, in the rare glades, among the trees that hid the sky and in the high ferns where they looked like swimmers. They seldom came near to one another, because they were few and the park was vast. But when chance brought one or more together, near enough for them to realize it had done so, then they hastened to turn back or, without going to such extremes, simply aside, as if ashamed to be seen by their fellows. But sometimes they brushed against one another without seeming to notice it, their heads buried in the ample hood.

Macmann carried with him and contemplated from time to time the photograph that Moll had given him, it was perhaps rather a daguerreotype. She was standing beside a chair and squeezing in her hands her long plaits. Traces were visible, behind her, of a kind of trellis with clambering flowers, roses probably, they sometimes like to clamber. When giving this keep-sake to Macmann she had said, I was fourteen, I well remember the day, a summer day, it was my birthday, afterwards they took me to see Punch and Judy. Macmann remembered those words. What he liked best in this picture was the chair, the seat of which seemed to be made of straw. Diligently Moll pressed her lips together, in order to hide her great buck-teeth. The roses must have been pretty, they must have scented the air. In the end Macmann tore up this photograph and threw the bits in the air, one windy day. Then they scattered, though all subjected to the same conditions, as though with alacrity.

When it rained, when it snowed

On. One morning Lemuel, putting in the prescribed appearance in the great hall before setting out on his rounds, found pinned on the board a notice concerning him. Group Lemuel, excursion to the islands, weather permitting, with Lady Pedal, leaving one p.m. His colleagues observed him, sniggering and poking one another in the ribs. But they did not dare say anything. One woman however did pass a witty remark, to good effect. Lemuel was not liked, that was clear. But would he have wished to be, that is less clear. He initialed the notice and went away. The sun was dragging itself up, dispatching on its way what perhaps would be, thanks to it, a glorious May or April day, April more likely, it is doubtless the Easter week-end, spent by Jesus in hell. And it may well have been in honor of this latter that Lady Pedal had organized, for the benefit of Lemuel's group, this outing to the islands which was going to cost her dear, but she was well off and lived for doing good and bringing a little happiness into the lives of those less fortunate than herself, who was all right in her head and to whom life had always smiled or, as she had it herself, returned her smile, enlarged as in a convex mirror, or a concave, I forget. Taking advantage of the terrestrial atmosphere that dimmed its brightness Lemuel glared with loathing at the sun. He had reached his room, on the fourth or fifth floor, whence on countless occasions he could have thrown himself in perfect safety out of the window if he had been less weak-minded. The long silver carpet was in position, ending in a point, trembling across the calm repoussé sea. The room was small and absolutely empty, for Lemuel slept on the bare boards and even off them ate his lesser meals, now at one place, now at another. But what matter about Lemuel and his room? On. Lady Pedal was not the only one to take an interest in the inmates of

111

Saint John of God's, known pleasantly locally as the Johnny Goddams, or the Goddam Johnnies, not the only one to treat them on an average once every two years to excursions by land and sea through scenery renowned for its beauty or grandeur and even to entertainments on the premises such as whole evenings of prestidigitation and ventriloquism in the moonlight on the terrace, no, but she was seconded by other ladies sharing her way of thinking and similarly blessed in means and leisure. But what matter about Lady Pedal? On. Carrying in one hand two buckets wedged the one within the other Lemuel proceeded to the vast kitchen, full of stir and bustle at that hour. Six excursion soups, he growled. What? said the cook. Six excursion soups! roared Lemuel, dashing his buckets against the oven, without however relinquishing the handles, for he retained enough presence of mind to dread the thought of having to stoop and pick them up again. The difference between an excursion soup and a common or house soup was simply this, that the latter was uniformly liquid whereas the former contained a piece of fat bacon intended to keep up the strength of the excursionist until his return. When his bucket had been filled Lemuel withdrew to a secluded place, rolled up his sleeve to the elbow, fished up from the bottom of the bucket one after another the six pieces of bacon, his own and the five others, ate all the fat off them, sucked the rinds and threw them back in the soup. Strange when you come to think of it, but after all not so strange really, that they should have issued six extra or excursion soups at his mere demand, without requiring a written order. The cells of the five were far apart and so astutely disposed that Lemuel had never been able to determine how best, that is to say with the minimum of fatigue and annoyance, to visit them in turn. In the first a young man, dead young, seated in an old rocking-chair, his shirt rolled up and his hands on his thighs, would have seemed asleep had not his eyes been wide open. He never went out, unless commanded to do so, and then someone had to accompany him, in order to make him move forward. His chamber-pot was empty, whereas in his bowl the soup of the previous day had congealed. The reverse would have been less surprising. But Lemuel was used to this, so used that he had long since ceased to wonder on what this creature fed. He emptied the bowl into his empty bucket and from his full bucket filled it with fresh soup. Then he went, a bucket in each hand, whereas up to now a single hand had been enough to carry the two buckets. Because of the excursion he locked the door behind him, an unnecessary precaution. The second cell, four or five hundred paces distant from the first, contained one whose only really striking features were his stature, his stiffness and his air of perpetually looking for something while at the same time wondering what that something could possibly be. Nothing in his person gave any indication of his age, whether he was marvellously well-preserved or on the contrary prematurely decayed. He was called the Saxon, though he was far from being any such thing. Without troubling to take off his shirt he had swathed himself in his two blankets as in swaddlings and over and above this rough and ready cocoon he wore his cloak. He gathered it shiveringly about him, with one hand, for he needed the other to help him in his investigation of all that aroused his suspicions. Good-morning, good-morning, good-morning, he said, with a strong foreign accent and darting fearful glances all about him, fucking awful business this, no, yes? Sudden starts instantly repressed dislodged him imperceptibly from his coign of maximum vantage in the centre of the room. What! he exclaimed. His soup, examined drop by drop, had been transferred in its entirety to his pot. Anxiously he watched Lemuel performing his office, filling and emptying. Dreamt all night of that bloody man Quin again, he said. It was his habit to go out from time to time, into the air. But after a few steps he would halt, totter, turn and hasten back into his cell, aghast at such depths of opacity.

In the third a small thin man was pacing up and down, his cloak folded over his arm, an umbrella in his hand. Fine head of white flossy hair. He was asking himself questions in a low voice, reflecting, replying. The door had hardly opened when he made a dart to get out, for he spent his days ranging about the park in all directions. Without putting down his buckets Lemuel sent him flying with a toss of his shoulder. He lay where he had fallen, clutching his cloak and umbrella. Then, having recovered from his surprise, he began to cry. In the fourth a misshapen giant, bearded, occupied to the exclusion of all else in scratching himself, intermittently. Sprawling on his pillow on the floor under the window, his head sunk, his mouth open, his legs wide apart, his knees raised, leaning with one hand on the ground while the other came and went under his shirt, he awaited his soup. When his bowl had been filled he stopped scratching and stretched out his hand towards Lemuel, in the daily disappointed hope of being spared the trouble of getting up. He still loved the gloom and secrecy of the ferns, but never sought them out. The youth then, the Saxon, the thin one and the giant. I don't know if they have changed, I don't remember. May the others forgive me. In the fifth Macmann, half asleep.

A few lines to remind me that I too subsist. He has not come back. How long ago is it now? I don't know. Long. And I? Indubitably going, that's all that matters. Whence this assurance? Try and think. I can't. Grandiose suffering. I am swelling. What if I should burst? The ceiling rises and falls, rises and falls, rhythmically, as when I was a foetus. Also to be mentioned a noise of rushing water, phenomenon mutatis mutandis perhaps analogous to that of the mirage, in the desert. The window. I shall not see it again. Why? Because, to my grief, I cannot turn my head. Leaden light again, thick, eddying, riddled with little tunnels through to brightness, perhaps I should say air, sucking air. All is ready. Except me. I am being given, if I may venture the expression, birth to into death, such is my impression. The feet are clear already, of the great cunt of existence. Favorable presentation I trust. My head will be the last to die.

Haul in your hands. I can't. The render rent. My story ended I'll be living yet. Promising lag. That is the end of me. I shall say I no more.

Surrounded by his little flock which after nearly two hours of efforts he had succeeded in assembling, single-handed, Pat having refused to help him, Lemuel stood on the terrace waiting for Lady Pedal to arrive. Cords tethered by the ankles the thin one to the youth, the Saxon to the giant, and Lemuel held Macmann by the arm. Of the five it was Macmann, furious at having been shut up in his cell all morning and at a loss to understand what was wanted of him, whose resistance had been the most lively. He had notably refused to stir a step without his hat, with such fierce determination that Lemuel had finally consented to his keeping it on, provided it was hidden by the hood. In spite of this Macmann continued peevish and agitated, trying to free his arm and saying over and over again, Let me go! Let me go! The youth, tormented by the sun, was grabbing feebly at the thin one's umbrella, saying, Pasol! Pasol! The thin one retaliated with petulant taps on his hands and arms. Naughty! he cried. Help! The giant had thrown his arms round the Saxon's neck and hung there, his legs limp. The Saxon, tottering, too proud to collapse, demanded to be enlightened in tones without anger. Who is this shite anyhow, he said, any of you poor buggers happen to know? The director, or his delegate, also present, said dreamily from time to time, Now, now, please. They were alone on the great terrace. Can it be she fears a change of weather? said the director. He added, turning towards Lemuel, I am asking you a question. The sky was cloudless, the air still. Where is the beautiful young man with the Messiah beard? But in that case would she not have telephoned? said the director.

The waggonette. Up on the box, beside the coachman, Lady Pedal. On one of the seats, set parallel to the wheels, Lemuel, Macmann, the Saxon and the giant. On the other, facing them, the youth, the thin one and two colossi dressed in sailor-suits. As they passed through the gates the children cheered. A sudden descent, long and steep, sent them plunging towards the sea. Under the drag of the brakes the wheels slid more than they rolled and the stumbling horses reared against the thrust. Lady Pedal clung to the box, her bust flung back. She was a huge, big, tall, fat woman. Artificial daisies with brilliant yellow disks gushed from her broad-brimmed straw hat. At the same time behind the heavily spotted fall-veil her plump red face appeared to pullulate. The passengers, yielding with unanimous inertia to the tilt of the seats, sprawled pell-mell beneath the box. Sit back! cried Lady Pedal. Nobody stirred. What good would that do? said one of the sailors. None, said the other. Should they not all get down, said Lady Pedal to the coachman, and walk? When they were safely at the bottom of the hill at last Lady Pedal turned affably to her guests. Courage my hearties! she said, to show she was not superior. The waggonette jolted on with gathering speed. The giant lay on the boards, between the seats. Are you the one in charge? said Lady Pedal. One of the sailors leaned towards Lemuel and said, She wants to know if you're the one in charge. Fuck off, said Lemuel. The Saxon uttered a roar which Lady Pedal, on the qui vive for the least sign of animation, was pleased to interpret as a manifestation of joy. That's the spirit! she cried. Sing! Make the most of this glorious day! Banish your cares, for an hour or so! And she burst forth:

> Oh the jolly jolly spring
> Blue and sun and nests and flowers
> Alleluiah Christ is King
> Oh the happy happy hours
> Oh the jolly jolly —

She broke off, discouraged. What is the matter with them? she said. The youth, less youthful now, doubled in two, his head swathed in the skirts of his cloak, seemed to be vomiting. His legs, monstrously bony and knock-kneed, were knocking to-

116

gether at the knees. The thin one, shivering, though in theory the Saxon is the shiverer, had resumed his dialogue. Motionless and concentrated between the voices he reinforced these with passionate gestures amplified by the umbrella. And you? . . . Thanks . . . And you? . . . THANKS! . . . True . . . Left . . . Try . . . Back . . . Where? . . . On . . . No! . . . Right . . . Try . . . Do you smell the sea, said Lady Pedal, I do. Macmann made a bid for freedom. In vain. Lemuel produced a hatchet from under his cloak and dealt himself a few smart blows on the skull, with the heel, for safety. Nice jaunt we're having, said one of the sailors. Swell, said the other. Sun azure. Ernest, hand out the buns, said Lady Pedal.

The boat. Room, as in the waggonette, for twice as many, three times, four times, at a pinch. A land receding, another approaching, big and little islands. No sound save the oars, the rowlocks, the blue sea against the keel. In the stern-sheets Lady Pedal, sad. What beauty! she murmured. Alone, not understood, good, too good. Taking off her glove she trailed in the transparent water her sapphire-laden hand. Four oars, no rudder, the oars steer. My creatures, what of them? Nothing. They are there, each as best he can, as best he can be somewhere. Lemuel watches the mountains rising behind the steeples beyond the harbor, no they are no more

No, they are no more than hills, they raise themselves gently, faintly blue, out of the confused plain. It was there somewhere he was born, in a fine house, of loving parents. Their slopes are covered with ling and furze, its hot yellow bells, better known as gorse. The hammers of the stone-cutters ring all day like bells.

The island. A last effort. The islet. The shore facing the open sea is jagged with creeks. One could live there, perhaps happy, if life was a possible thing, but nobody lives there. The deep water comes washing into its heart, between high walls of rock.

One day nothing will remain of it but two islands, separated by a gulf, narrow at first, then wider and wider as the centuries slip by, two islands, two reefs. It is difficult to speak of man, under such conditions. Come, Ernest, said Lady Pedal, let us find a place to picnic. And you, Maurice, she added, stay by the dinghy. She called that a dinghy. The thin one chafed to run about, but the youth had thrown himself down in the shade of a rock, like Sordello, but less noble, for Sordello resembled a lion at rest, and clung to it with both hands. The poor creatures, said Lady Pedal, let them loose. Maurice made to obey. Keep off, said Lemuel. The giant had refused to leave the boat, so that the Saxon could not leave it either. Macmann was not free either, Lemuel held him by the waist, perhaps lovingly. Well, said Lady Pedal, you are the one in charge. She moved away with Ernest. Suddenly she turned and said, You know, on the island, there are Druid

remains. She looked at them in turn. When we have had our tea, she said, we shall hunt for them, what do you say? Finally she moved away again, followed by Ernest carrying the hamper in his arms. When she had disappeared Lemuel released Macmann, went up behind Maurice who was sitting on a stone filling his pipe and killed him with the hatchet. We're getting on, getting on. The youth and the giant took no notice. The thin one broke his umbrella against the rock, a curious gesture. The Saxon cried, bending forward and slapping his thighs, Nice work, sir, nice work! A little later Ernest came back to fetch them. Going to meet him Lemuel killed him in his turn, in the same way as the other. It merely took a little longer. Two decent, quiet, harmless men, brothers-in-law into the bargain, there are billions of such brutes. Macmann's huge head. He has put his hat on again. The voice of Lady Pedal, calling. She appeared, joyous. Come along, she cried, all of you, before the tea gets cold. But at the sight of the late sailors she fainted, which caused her to fall. Smash her! screamed the Saxon. She had raised her veil and was holding in her hand a tiny sandwich. She must have broken something in her fall, her hip perhaps, old ladies often break their hips, for no sooner had she recovered her senses than she began to moan and groan, as if she were the only being on the face of the earth deserving of pity. When the sun had vanished, behind the hills, and the lights of the land began to glitter, Lemuel made Macmann and the two others get into the boat and got into it himself. Then they set out, all six, from the shore.

Gurgles of outflow.

This tangle of grey bodies is they. Silent, dim, perhaps clinging to one another, their heads buried in their cloaks, they lie together in a heap, in the night. They are far out in the bay. Lemuel has shipped his oars, the oars trail in the water. The night is strewn with absurd

absurd lights, the stars, the beacons, the buoys, the lights of earth and in the hills the faint fires of the blazing gorse. Macmann, my last, my possessions, I remember, he is there too, perhaps he sleeps. Lemuel

Lemuel is in charge, he raises his hatchet on which the blood will never dry, but not to hit anyone, he will not hit anyone, he will not hit anyone any more, he will not touch anyone any more, either with it or with it or with it or with or

or with it or with his hammer or with his stick or with his fist or in thought in dream I mean never he will never

or with his pencil or with his stick or

119

or light light I mean

never there he will never

never anything

there

any more